AND DANGEROUS TO KNOW

AND DANGEROUS TO KNOW

Elizabeth Daly

FELONY & MAYHEM PRESS • NEW YORK

All the characters and events portrayed in this work are fictitious.

AND DANGEROUS TO KNOW

A Felony & Mayhem mystery

PRINTING HISTORY

First edition (Rinehart): 1949
Felony & Mayhem edition: 2015

ISBN: 978-1-63194-062-0

Manufactured in the United States of America

Library of Congress Cataloging-in-Publication Data

Daly, Elizabeth, 1878-1967.
And dangerous to know / Elizabeth Daly.
pages cm. -- (A Felony & Mayhem mystery)
"First edition (Rinehart): 1949" -- Verso title page.
Previously published: New York ; Toronto : Rinehart & Company, Inc., ©1949. A Murray Hill mystery.
Includes bibliographical references.
ISBN 978-1-63194-062-0
1. Gamadge, Henry (Fictitious character)--Fiction. 2. Book collectors--Fiction. 3. Missing persons--Fiction. 4. New York (N.Y.) --Fiction. I. Title.
PS3507.A4674A53 2015
813'.54--dc23

2015019198

CONTENTS

The icon above says you're holding a copy of a book in the Felony & Mayhem "Vintage" category. These books were originally published prior to about 1965, and feature the kind of twisty, ingenious puzzles beloved by fans of Agatha Christie and John Dickson Carr. If you enjoy this book, you may well like other "Vintage" titles from Felony & Mayhem Press.

AND DANGEROUS TO KNOW

CHAPTER ONE

Interior

THERE ARE STILL a few such rows of old brownstone houses on the upper East Side in New York, and among the bright remodelled dwellings and the glossy apartments that hem them in, they look rather grim. Some of their high stoops and deep areas are in bad repair or not cared for at all, since these belong to rooming-houses or to property that is boarded-up, for rent or for sale, waiting for an estate to be settled or an absentee landlord to die.

But among these relics there are still living fossils, private residences with well-swept doorways, where window boxes bloom all spring and summer; people like the Dunbars live in them, people who have plenty of money but are careful about spending it, who have a strong attachment to the past and dislike change and novelty. They bring their plumbing and their kitchens up to date, and go comfortably on where their grandparents were comfortable three-quarters of a century ago.

The Dunbar house was pleasantly situated on the south side of the block and just off the park, and in summer it had dark blue Holland shades in the windows, and a caretaker to water the geraniums in the window boxes while the family was away. But on this twenty-second of July the shades were up and the storm doors open. The family was at home.

At about one o'clock Miss Alice Dunbar climbed the front stoop and rang the bell. She was in her early thirties, of medium height, and thin. Her complexion was sallow, her hair and eyes dark, her face quite without expression. She was wearing conservative and expensive clothing: a dark blue voile dress, a small dark blue hat, fawn kid gloves, black shoes.

Her blank look was not a look of indifference; there was nothing calm about it. It might have meant a deliberate withdrawal into herself, the tension of long years of defence. It did not express passivity. Waiting for the door to open, she glanced to the right towards the dusty trees of the park, to the left, past a vacant lot, towards Madison Avenue; but her dark eyes saw nothing. She was preoccupied with her own thoughts.

A maid opened the door. Miss Dunbar asked: "Am I late, Eileen?"

"Just on time, Miss."

"I hope there's iced tea."

"Iced coffee, Miss."

"Oh. Good," said Miss Dunbar vaguely. She climbed the two flights of stairs to her bedroom.

When she came back, without her gloves and hat, her family were at table in the dining-room: Mr. Dunbar, Mrs. Dunbar, and their widowed younger daughter, Mrs. Richfield Tanner. Mr. Angus Dunbar was a man of sixty-five, thin everywhere—a narrow head, a thin long nose, a thin mouth. He had a certain amount of dry humour, which Mrs. Dunbar appreciated, but it would hardly be an exaggeration to say that she never laughed. When amused, she smiled. She was pink-faced and blond, a little plump, and she sat up straight in her chair.

Abigail Tanner had lost her husband, a flying man, in the war. Blond like her mother, she had been a very pretty girl; now she had lost her fresh colouring, and looked a little dissipated. Her father and mother did not see the change like that;

they said she had been through so much it had aged her. She had her husband's money, and in winter-time she lived alone in a hotel. This summer she had been with her family in their cottage on Cape Cod, and had come to the city with them for a funeral. The funeral, that of an aged relative, had taken place the week before, but Mr. Dunbar was staying on as executor of the estate.

Alice came in and sat down opposite her sister. Her brown hair was in a low pompadour, and wisps escaped from it. She looked very tired.

Her mother said: "Why is it, I wonder, that the rest of us can always be in time for meals."

Alice said nothing; she began on the jellied bouillon the maid put before her. After a pause her father observed: "I think your mother spoke to you, Alice."

"Yes, Father; did she? I'm sorry if I was ten seconds late."

"Well, really," said Mrs. Dunbar in her rather high voice.

"I suddenly remembered another errand. Stockings for the shore."

"Where?" asked Mrs. Dunbar, always interested in shopping.

"Just a little place."

"It's a waste of money to go to those shops."

Abigail, her elbows on the table, languidly eating celery, said that she'd go without stockings at the shore and in town too, if she had to go errands in this heat.

"Alice was getting things for me this morning," replied Mrs. Dunbar.

"I still think we might have given the funeral a miss," said Abigail. "In the circumstances, I mean." She smiled. "Don't you, Father? Why should we bother?"

Mr. Dunbar answered indulgently: "Wouldn't have done. Your great-aunt! No other family to go."

"But my goodness, to open the house!"

"Your father will be here for a good while," said Mrs. Dunbar, "with all the estate business to settle. His comfort comes first. Do you think I should allow him to be all by himself at the club?"

"Your poor children could have stayed at the Cape," said Mrs. Tanner, smiling at her mother.

"And keep two establishments going? Besides, it looked very much better for us to be here."

"Don't we get *anything* out of it, Father?"

"My executor's commission," replied Mr. Dunbar drily.

"We always expected Aunt Woodworth to leave a great deal to her charities," said Mrs. Dunbar.

"And we don't need the money. Quite right to leave it as she wished," said Mr. Dunbar.

"I know, but—" Mrs. Tanner looked across the table at her sister, who had seemed oblivious of the conversation. She asked: "You had plenty of time; why on earth didn't you go up there now and then?"

Alice replied: "I try not to go where I bore people. And I wasn't brought up to truckle for money; or was I?"

Mrs. Dunbar said: "Hush," as the maid came in, removed cups and brought salad. When they were alone again, she went on: "Decent attention is not truckling."

"Well, anyway," said Mrs. Tanner, "there weren't any legacies except for the servants; I was afraid she'd put in a codicil in favour of the protégés."

Mr. Dunbar laughed. "No, thank Heaven, nothing like that! Your great-aunt wasn't doddering."

"I had an idea she was," said Mrs. Tanner, laughing. "The way she went on about that convalescent ex-marine of hers, what was his name? Dobbs. And the others before. She talked about nothing else when we were there at Christmas."

"Cases from the hospital," said Mrs. Dunbar quickly. "Of course she would be interested. She lived for that hospital."

"Oh well, I suppose they got cash presents," said Mrs. Tanner.

"Nothing considerable," said her father. "Her accounts were very well kept. Mr. Baynes attended to them for her."

"Well then," said Mrs. Tanner idly, "I suppose none of the protégés pushed her downstairs. That's something."

"What on earth!" Mr. Dunbar, gazing at his daughter sternly, spoke in a tone of strong disapprobation.

"Just joking, Father."

"Gail," said Mrs. Dunbar in some agitation, "you must not speak so carelessly. Aunt was over eighty years of age, and she didn't fall downstairs. She had had a stroke before. She simply fell in the hall. There is no excuse for—"

"Oh please, Mother darling! I didn't mean it. I was just trying to be funny," said Abigail, her hand on her mother's arm.

Mr. Dunbar was still shocked. "A lawyer doesn't care for that kind of joke, Gail; unless he happens to be the wrong kind of lawyer, in which case you would find yourself in court answering to a charge of slander."

"Oh goodness."

Mrs. Dunbar, suddenly frowning, looked at her husband. "I suppose none of those young men would put in a claim of any kind, Angus?"

"Nonsense."

"You hear of such things."

"Impossible here."

"But it happens, after old people die, and it doesn't look well when the family refuses to pay."

Mr. Dunbar was really irritated. "These fellows were simply cases she heard of through the hospital, war cases. She had them out at her place sometimes for a little rest, or a good meal. One of them—this Dobbs—helped in the garden and with the car. I understand that they all have work now; perfectly respectable young men."

"Handsome young men," said Mrs. Tanner, laughing.

"Who says so?" asked Mrs. Dunbar.

"Aunt Woodworth said so; at least one of them was." She added, moving her salt-cellar about and looking at it, "By the way, talking of young men, would you two pets mind if I had a couple in this evening after dinner?"

Alice looked up at her sister, and then down at her plate again.

"Not at all, dear," said Mrs. Dunbar.

"You needn't meet them, don't bother," said Mrs. Tanner. "They're nobody you know, just friends of Richie's. Some of his squadron pals might seem a little rough to you. Just types from the wide-open spaces, nice boys, but you wouldn't quite understand them."

Mr. Dunbar said: "I suppose they won't break the furniture."

Alice said with a short laugh: "More likely to break the piano," and Gail cast a viperish look in her direction.

"Oh dear," said Mrs. Dunbar.

"It isn't the playing," said Mr. Dunbar, "it's what they play."

"And when they play," said Alice. "Excuse me; I take it back."

Her parents looked at her, puzzled; Abigail went on: "I really oughtn't to do this kind of thing to you dear people."

"But we never sit in the drawing-room," said Mrs. Dunbar. "It won't be a bother if they don't stay too late."

"I ought to go back to the Stanton," said Mrs. Tanner.

"No, no, darling. For such a short time! And it's so nice to have you here again."

"Cheers us all up," remarked Alice.

"At least your callers can't be accused of doing that." Mrs. Tanner smiled. "There used to be a word for them. What was it? Muffs?"

Mr. Dunbar leaned back in his chair to laugh. "I haven't heard that word for fifty years!"

"I picked it up in the R.A.F.," said Mrs. Tanner smugly.

The maid came in and began to clear the table for dessert. Mr. Dunbar, still laughing, said: "All very nice fellows. Now Arthur Jennings—quiet, but he's an excellent lawyer. Knows a lot about patent law."

Abigail said with affected pique: "But he's *my* gentleman friend, Father; I just lend him out sometimes."

Alice had flushed a little, but she did not carry on the fray with much interest. She said: "I'm always flattered, of course, to go out with him after you've refused the invitation. But I wish he didn't always insist on coming in afterwards. I get a little tired of his conversation."

Mrs. Dunbar said: "Sometimes we hear him droning on for half the night. What *do* you find to talk about?"

"He finds it." As if her contribution to the talk had been an effort, and had tired her, she sank against the back of her chair. The maid went out of the room with her tray. When she had gone Abigail addressed her father demurely: "Why don't you ask the muffs their intentions, Father? They've been hanging around for at least ten years."

Alice said absently: "Or Father might ask you your intentions. Rich has been dead four years—that's a long time."

Mrs. Tanner, very angry, cast her napkin on the table and seemed about to rise. She said: "I won't take this kind of thing."

Mrs. Dunbar said sharply: "No quarrelling, Alice. You know I can't stand it."

"I know," said Alice. "If I say anything, that's quarrelling."

"It takes two."

Alice burst out laughing. The maid came in with ice-cream, and had just finished passing the plates when the doorbell rang. She hurried out, and then there was a sound of giggling and whispering in the hall.

"What on earth," murmured Mr. Dunbar. Mrs. Dunbar was frowning heavily, but her face cleared when a young man came into the room.

Everybody turned to look at him. "Why Bruce," exclaimed Mrs. Dunbar and Mrs. Tanner together, and Mr. Dunbar was smiling too. Even Alice showed interest, but it was mingled with a certain irony.

The young man was very blond, light-haired and grey-eyed, with a faint look of Mr. Dunbar about him; but he was very good-looking, full of vitality, and with a natural gaiety that he had not inherited from any Dunbar. He went over to Mrs. Dunbar and kissed her cheek.

"Wha hae, wha hae, how's the clan? Dear Auntie Pibroch. And Uncle Haggis, and little Plaidie and Kiltie." He went around the table, shaking hands with Mr. Dunbar, kissing Abigail and Alice, sitting down at last in the chair between Mrs. Dunbar and Abigail that the maid, smiling, had pushed up for him. "No, no ice-cream, thanks. Iced coffee? Just what I need."

"But why so Scottish?" asked Mr. Dunbar, laughing.

"Well, I'm doing a genealogy for an old gentleman, he's looking for his clan. I don't know how I'm ever going to get him into the Highlands, unless"—his eyes fell on a stained-glass plaque let into the middle light of the window—"Alice might give me a hand. That was a job!" He laughed with whole-hearted amusement. "Alice, you'll have to help me; you're a whiz at bridging the gaps and blotting the 'scutcheons."

Mrs. Dunbar was unable to be cross with this privileged relative; but she said with dignity: "It's only what Alice found in the books, Brucey. My people really were—"

"I know, Auntie, I know. Alice, mind you do me my next Christmas card with my armorial bearings on it."

Abigail said: "You certainly seem to have found yourself a man-sized job this time, Brucey."

"Jobs? They pay for my real jobs—my tennis, you know, and picking the winners."

"Are you staying in town?" Mr. Dunbar was also indulgent towards the lively young man.

"Lord no, I just came up to see my tailor and so on. I'm driving back this afternoon, in fact right away."

"Driving!" exclaimed Abigail. "When on earth did you start from Washington?"

"Oh, in the small hours. That's when I like to drive in summer, and I'll get back in the cool of the night. Ever see the Pennsville Ferry at sunrise? Beautiful sight." He got his cigarette case out of his pocket, and looked at Mrs. Dunbar. She nodded. "Have one, anybody?"

Abigail took one, and he lighted it and his own.

"You're a very bad boy, you know," said Mrs. Dunbar affectionately. "You ought to have come on for the funeral."

"Well, Auntie, I never laid eyes on any Woodworth in my life, and I wasn't expecting a legacy."

"Neither were we," said Mr. Dunbar. "But families must show a united front on these occasions."

"I saw in the papers that she left everything to some hospital. Hanged if I'd have bothered to go in your place."

"I'm her executor, Bruce my boy."

"Is that a good thing to be?"

"I think her own lawyer, old Baynes, would have liked the job," said Mr. Dunbar with a quirk of his mouth.

"And Bruce," said Mrs. Dunbar, "you did lay eyes on Aunt Woodworth. Your mother took you there once when you were a little boy."

"I must have been a very little boy. I don't remember a thing about it. Well, she probably knew you don't need the money, but my God, why didn't somebody tell her I do?"

"You don't really, Bruce?" His aunt looked concerned for him.

"I get by. And they say it's just as expensive to live in Europe, so I think I'll stay on here after all."

"I'm glad of that."

"Do you miss it frightfully, Bruce?" asked Abigail.

"That's a foolish question," said Mr. Dunbar. "Of course he misses it, and he misses his home."

"They certainly didn't leave much of the villa," said Bruce. He finished his coffee, stubbed out his cigarette. "My mother was well out of it—I'm glad she never lived to see that ash heap. I got a glimpse of it while I was back there on the staff."

"Too bad, too bad."

"Might be worse, mightn't it?" He got up.

"Why don't you come up to the Cape and stay with us, dear?" asked his aunt, while he kissed her.

"Just wait till I finish Mr. Gummy's fairy tale; I'll have him a lineal descendant of King Duncan before I'm through with him. He has wads of money; perhaps he'll send me to England to confer with Portcullis. Don't forget, Alice—paint me that Christmas card. How about a couple of winners, proper, supporting tennis balls quartered with highballs?"

When he had gone, and the front door had been heard to slam, Mrs. Dunbar sighed deeply.

"Poor boy; it was very sweet of him to drop in on us. Did he get anything at all out of France, dear?"

"Not a thing," said Mr. Dunbar. "But he has what his mother invested here. Quite enough for him. He could really do anything if he liked."

"I like him as he is," said Abigail.

"There's a word for *him*," said Alice. *"Faux bonhomme."*

"That's like you," said Abigail without looking at her. "Just like you."

"I have always found him candid and sincere," said Mr. Dunbar, glancing at his elder daughter in some surprise.

"I suppose he is. Yes, I think he is."

"And his high spirits are certainly not put on," said Mrs. Dunbar, rising.

They all rose. "No, they're not," agreed Alice.

"Then what did you mean?"

"I mean they don't mean anything." Alice Dunbar dismissed him, and the subject, with coldness and finality. She followed the others out of the room, and began to climb the stairs.

"Alice," said her mother.

"Yes?" She turned and looked over her shoulder, her hand on the balustrade.

"Gail says she is going out at five, and your father will be at his office until all hours. Don't plan to stay out yourself later than five, if you do go out again."

Alice smiled faintly. "I ought to be back by then; but if I don't come, there are three servants."

"Your father doesn't wish me to be alone in the house with the servants."

The sound of the piano came from the drawing-room. Alice said: "If Gail can find a party to go to at this time of the year, perhaps I could."

"Nonsense, your friends are not in town."

"There's that."

She went on up the two flights of stairs; there was a pinched look about her face as she turned into her bedroom at the back of the house.

CHAPTER TWO

Bargains

ALICE DUNBAR CLOSED the door behind her. She stood for a few moments leaning her shoulder against it, her hand still on the knob; she felt herself trembling a little, and waited as she was until she had controlled that absurd chattering of the teeth and had stiffened her knees. Then she turned and walked firmly across the room and sat down in front of the low dressing-table.

It was a girl's room, hardly changed from the day when she had been promoted to it from the nursery. Pink walls, white woodwork, iridescent pink tiles enclosing the gas log fire, maple furniture, Dresden ornaments on the mantelpiece. Pictures in maple frames—flower pieces. One of them was an early effort of her own, a watercolour and an awful daub, she knew very well. But it always got rehung after the walls were repainted.

The curtains and the old-rose rug had been put away for the summer, and their absence gave the room a pleasantly bare look; as if it were ready for a change. But in the autumn the pink curtains would go up again, the imperishable rug go down.

She sat looking at herself closely in the glass. Not bad features, she had never been able to see anything much wrong with them. Baffled by that problem as always, she turned her eyes away from herself and opened a drawer. She took out a large black handbag with a wide, stiff base, which seemed well-filled already. She transferred a few things to it from her other bag, the one she had carried that morning; a compact, a plain handkerchief, a purse with clean notes in it.

She got up, took the small plain hat off the bed and put it on, pulled her gloves on, picked up the handbag, and stood looking about her; seeing nothing, merely thinking whether she had forgotten something. Then she went quietly out into the hall.

The house was silent; all the way downstairs there was not a sound. Her mother would be in her room, her father reading in the upstairs sitting-room—unless he had gone to his office. Not that it mattered. She opened the front door and went out, slammed the great walnut-and-glass bulwark behind her, and descended the steps. Turning left, she walked to Fifth Avenue; turning left again, she went south for several blocks; then she crossed to the park side.

She waited for a bus, boarded it, and settled herself next to a window as for a long ride. She got off at a busy corner in the midtown shopping district, and stood surprised at the crowds; Alice Dunbar had had a vague idea that there were very few people in New York in summer. The Friday afternoon bustle astonished her.

She entered a department store, looking about her as if she was unfamiliar with it, but asking no questions. After a while she found a stocking counter, a table where boxes of stockings were displayed at a reduction. She pushed through the crowd, found a pair of stockings that would fit her, and got hold of a salesgirl. The things were an ugly light colour, and would not last long, but she saw many just like them on the legs that went past in droves up and down the aisles.

A little farther on, at a cosmetics counter, she bought a compact of a lighter powder than her own carefully blended brand, and bright lipstick. The girl was too busy to help her, so she found rouge for herself, thrusting her arm between other women to get it. She held out her hand with the things in it, and they were snatched from her and wrapped. She had to wait for her change.

She fought her way out of the store, crossed the avenue, and went into another bigger place. Here she found a counter where hats were being sold—mere strips of ribbon and cheap flowers. She bought one, and on her way out, a white muslin collar worked with machine-made embroidery. At a near-by ten cent store, she bought a paper shopping bag and put her parcels into it.

On the avenue again, she crossed and took a bus downtown. She got out and walked to a huge emporium which she had often heard of but never seen. Here she acquired a pair of fabric gloves, thick and white; gilt earrings, fastened to a card; and a transparent red raincoat off a rack. Then she went up in the elevator to the ladies' room.

It was a big place with cross-aisles, and no attendant in sight. She shut herself into a cubicle, changed her stockings, changed her hat, put on the earrings, and, as well as she could without a mirror, adjusted the collar. Afterwards, at one of the long row of mirrors, she fastened the collar more firmly and began to make up. When she had finished she half smiled at the figure in the glass; by her own standards she looked like a clown, but no more clownish than the faces around her; and there was a certain haggard handsomeness about her that she had certainly never had before.

She slipped on the mackintosh, leaving it open. A warm day to be wearing any coat, but perhaps the kind of suburbanite she had turned into would carry one from the end of some mysterious subway line, in case of a thunderstorm, and wear it for convenience.

Would anybody recognize her now? Not her own parents. She had changed more than her appearance, she had changed her whole personality.

Her handbag under her arm, her shopping bag in her white-gloved hand, she went down in the elevator and out into the street. She found an up-town subway station, and stood aghast; shoppers were already making for home. But she finally allowed herself to be swept down the stairs, dropped her dime in the turnstile, and pushed her way into the local that was standing there as if actually waiting for her. The doors closed her in, the lights of the station moved past, there was a roar, and they were in the dark.

CHAPTER THREE

Sheltered Life

"**OFF THE MAP**," said Macloud. "Right off the map."

It was Sunday, August the fourteenth. Gamadge and his old coloured servant Theodore were keeping house together for the few days that Gamadge had to be in New York on business, and Macloud the lawyer had invited himself to dinner. They sat in the library, facing each other in one of the long windows. There was coffee on a table between them, and they were smoking.

"I've been in the country until this week," said Gamadge. "I only know what I saw in the papers, and you know what it's like among the bees and the flowers. You simply don't get all the details. But it's an extraordinary case. I wondered how deep you'd be in it."

"I'm a partner of old Angus Dunbar's, as you know, and I was in town on the Woodworth Estate business; the aunt, you remember? She died the week before, and Dunbar was sole executor. They called me up that night—the evening of the day the girl disappeared. I persuaded them to set the police on it and start the Bureau of Missing Persons going. Mrs. Dunbar, poor thing, would have liked to keep it quiet a little longer, till we'd tried the hospitals; but Dunbar saw my point and didn't wait. She must have left the house soon after lunch, not much after two o'clock—a parcel came for her at a quarter past, something she bought that morning, and she was gone by that time. Mrs. Dunbar expected her back by five, but wasn't really worried until dinner time. At eight o'clock Dunbar called me. Six hours." Macloud shook his head. "Into space in six hours."

Gamadge said: "And now it's twenty-three days. Well, if means of communication have improved, so have means of transportation."

"But nowadays you can do a lot of eliminating," said Macloud. "And the search was nation-wide in twelve hours, and world-wide in not much more than twenty-four. Not a trace. The police say she must have gone voluntarily, but they usually do say that."

"Most people do."

"Give them an elopement every time. But she took nothing but what she stood up in, not even a top-coat; and she can't have had much money with her—the remains of her July allowance. She didn't spend much, her clothes went on her mother's accounts."

Gamadge said: "I suppose there wasn't anything the papers didn't get?"

"Gamadge, I swear there wasn't a thing. I was on the spot, I talked to them all—the Dunbars, and the other daughter, Abigail Tanner. If you're thinking of a kidnapping, that's out; the family never got any ransom letter."

"But accidental death, or murder, does sometimes occur during a kidnapping—as we all know."

"Yes, and the ransom note comes, just the same." Macloud shook his head again, frowning. "And it was early in the afternoon on a summer's day. A shopping tour!"

"I admit it doesn't seem likely," said Gamadge. Theodore came in, took away the coffee set, and placed a tray with whisky and glasses on the table. As Gamadge mixed the drinks, Macloud went on:

"And a woman of that type wouldn't deliberately walk into anything, Gamadge. I've met her, you know. Quiet, repressed girl, over thirty years old. Rather dull. I can hardly imagine an elopement, and I certainly can't imagine a reason for one. Now suicide—"

Gamadge handed Macloud his tumbler. "That likely?" he asked.

"I shouldn't say so, but what do we know about anybody's mind? Even families don't know. I suppose she can't have had a particularly happy life."

"No?"

"Well, there was a broken engagement ten years ago, and she doesn't seem to have had much to do, outside the usual social round, except a little puttering with art. She designed Christmas cards and gift cards and—er—wastebaskets. That kind of thing. And for the last five years her mother's been more or less laid up with high blood pressure. Abigail doesn't live at home, so most of the responsibility fell on Alice. But a good many people have a worse time than that, and manage to stay alive. And the family say they saw no signs of depression. That last day at lunch—the maid says she was laughing; laughed at least twice during the meal. The cousin, Bruce Dunbar, was there. I talked to him, so did the police."

"I remember that there was a cousin there that day."

"Only for a few minutes. But he knew them all, and I thought he might have some ideas—as a bystander. He's an amusing fellow; lives in Washington. He's only been in this country a year since childhood—his father was attached to various embassies, and their headquarters were in or near Paris. He was a staff interpreter during the war, knows about six languages. He was meant for diplomacy himself, but he's rather uprooted. It's a family joke—he's always inventing ridiculous jobs he says he's got. Well, this Bruce Dunbar says Alice was just as usual that day while he was there, perhaps a little quieter than usual, that's all. He says she was anything but an unstable type, so far as he can judge—in fact, the contrary."

Gamadge drank some whisky. He said: "I suppose her friends were investigated."

Macloud laughed shortly. "Even the ones that went to Europe. As for her men friends, poor devils—I saw most of them myself. She had two or three reliable old relics from her younger days; one of them is Jennings; remember Artie Jennings?"

"Our classmate; yes, I know Artie."

"Is *he* a blameless type? They're all like that. They were grilled, and so was the unfortunate ex-fiancé. He hasn't seen her since the engagement was broken; he's married and has five children and lives in Michigan. He couldn't have been near New York, and it doesn't look as if she'd gone to Michigan. The papers even got hold of a little art teacher that supervised Alice Dunbar's art work. She was on vacation in Vermont, running an art class; but Alice Dunbar didn't go to Woodstock, Vermont. As for her women friends, she had no intimates; just old schoolmates and so on that she went to bridge parties and theatre parties with, in a crowd."

Gamadge said: "Evidently not much contact with the underworld."

"No. And no marriage, either."

Gamadge raised his eyebrows.

"Decide for yourself," said Macloud, "whether she had a chance to establish residence anywhere outside our bailiwick; and here—they haven't missed a thing, Gamadge. They've been at it more than three weeks."

"I don't know what chance she had. You mean she led what's known as the sheltered life?"

Macloud leaned forward and pointed the stem of his pipe at Gamadge. "She literally hadn't *time* to make any detours."

"You mean that?" Gamadge was mildly astonished.

Macloud sat back. "Let me tell you." He waited while Theodore replenished the ice bowl, and lighted lamps. Then he got his pipe going, and went on:

"The Dunbars are conservative people. Abigail Tanner cut loose; she married Richfield Tanner, who was not conservative, but who was such a good match that the Dunbars gave their blessing. The marriage emancipated Abigail; she lives in a suite at the Stanton."

"The Stanton's conservative enough," remarked Gamadge.

"Yes, but she's there, and she lives her own life. She was with the family on Cape Cod, by the way, when old Mrs. Ames Woodworth died; came down with them for the funeral. That's why she was with them at the house on the twenty-second of July.

"Well, since Mrs. Dunbar's semi-invalidism, Alice seems to have had no private life at all. Alice has been nurse-companion, housekeeper, secretary, and telephone girl. After breakfast, in town or country, she and her mother went for a drive and a shopping round; they've got an old chauffeur they swear by. Then lunch. Then some charity board, still with her mother, or perhaps some party; but the car would take her there and bring her home on the dot. She was put down at this art teacher's studio on Thursdays, and picked up afterwards. She was never on the street after dark. If she was a minute late, there was hell to pay. Do you see what I mean?"

"I'm beginning to get it. How about the chauffeur?"

"Forget him. Abigail tells me he's a grumpy old customer, very disobliging to the younger members of the family; he wouldn't have taken them around the block without orders from higher up. I admit," said Macloud, "that Alice was allowed out of an evening now and then with one of the boyfriends. Theatre, a concert. But in the family car."

"The Dunbar car?"

"Certainly the Dunbar car."

"Don't tell me things like that," said Gamadge. "I can't take them."

"My dear fellow, don't you know what happens to people who drive around in taxis? They get into collisions, and if they're not killed they have to appear in court as a witness to the accident. They catch diseases. Or they're taken for a ride and robbed of their jewellery and knocked on the head."

"I see."

"And the boyfriends were not likely to conspire with Alice in sampling the gay life. I'll give you their names."

"Don't; I'd rather not hear them."

"And Jennings wasn't really Alice's friend, he's an old suitor of Abigail's; faithful as a burr on a tweed coat. He took Alice out if Abigail couldn't or wouldn't go." Macloud threw himself back in his chair. "Now tell me how Alice Dunbar managed to cook up a love affair in those circumstances; or get married, or even meet a stranger."

Gamadge said: "I'm coming around to the suicide theory."

"Well, as to the effect on her, Abigail says she didn't seem to mind. Since the broken engagement—I'm afraid the man did walk out on her, though of course the family said it was mutual—since then she doesn't seem to have shown much interest. But Abigail frankly admits that she and Alice were not intimate. They lived entirely separate lives, and Alice hardly went down to the Stanton to lunch or tea more than a couple of times a year. And she only went then because Mrs. Dunbar sent her—Mrs. Dunbar wouldn't permit a feud or an estrangement between the daughters."

Gamadge pondered. "The unfortunate girl seems to have been out on her own that Friday she disappeared."

"Yes, the bars were down that week, they hadn't the car. Routine shattered. But you don't engineer a final getaway like hers in a few days." He added: "A few hours out of a few days. She was on the job at home as usual."

"The sister was out that afternoon, wasn't she?"

"Yes, having cocktails with a friend of hers, a Mrs. Lynch, who was passing through town. You don't think the police missed any tricks, do you?"

"No, I suppose not. Bruce Dunbar, for instance—Alice knew *him*."

"She wasn't at his place in Washington at six the next morning." Macloud added sombrely: "Dead or alive. He was considered a very suspicious character, you know; lives alone at present in a little house in Washington, and has a garage. But why..." Macloud brooded. "Why! You find me a motive—for getting her out of the way, for killing her. Any motive at all. Money's out—she had none of her own, and how could anybody cash in on it if she had a million?"

"She didn't inherit from the aunt that died?"

"No, and didn't expect to. Mrs. Woodworth left everything except legacies to servants away from the family; to the Aaron Means Hospital, which her husband helped to found. The Dunbars knew her intentions."

"When did the old lady die?"

"Let's see: Sunday, July tenth. The funeral was on the thirteenth."

"How much did she leave?"

"About a million."

"You think in millions, Macloud. Fatalities tread on one another's heels in the Dunbar family, don't they?"

"Old Mrs. Woodworth's death wasn't a tragedy for them; they saw very little of her, and she was over eighty and had had a stroke before. High time she went, if you ask me."

"We can't ask her," said Gamadge, smiling.

"They're very clannish," said Macloud. "They all came down for the funeral; came down on the eleventh, I think. They were going back to the Cape as soon as Dunbar got the Woodworth affairs in shape. She had her own lawyer, old Baynes, and he handed the whole thing over to us on a platter—not a nickel out." Macloud laughed. "Abigail says they were a little worried, the old lady had been getting interested in some war protégés; cases from the hospital. They were afraid there might be big largesse for them in the will, and a scandal. But no; if the boys got anything it wasn't enough to make old Baynes raise an eyebrow."

"She might have adopted one of them."

"She didn't. The last favourite was a young fellow named Dobbs, Walter Dobbs; he came to the funeral. He's happily established at present in Brooklyn somewhere."

"Died of another stroke, did she?"

"Yes, she was found in the front hall. At first they thought she might have fallen downstairs, but old people bruise easily on bare floors, and probably she just collapsed."

"Nobody seems to have profited much—unless the hospital sent someone to push her downstairs?"

Macloud laughed. "I don't think they were sorry to get the money, anyhow. They're going to have a new wing. Aren't you going to tell me what happened to Alice Dunbar, Gamadge?"

"I couldn't even make a guess."

"She wasn't a slummer, she couldn't have been blackmailed—never tried to raise money. How did she run into trouble on that July afternoon? If it was amnesia, and there's not a hint of it in her medical history, why hasn't she been picked up and turned in—there's a reward, and plenty of publicity! If some maniac killed her, why hide the body?"

"Only one reason—safety for the murderer. How many women have been killed to get rid of them?"

"But my God, Gamadge, why should any man want to get rid of Alice Dunbar? She was a catch; she would have inherited from her parents."

"If they didn't like the man?"

"Everybody knew her circumstances. An ineligible would know what he could expect. If they had to keep the affair a secret, he'd know damn well!"

"People change their minds."

"Well, suppose she was hanging on to him; in their station of life—or hers—the man would merely quit; like that first fellow she was engaged to. And in these days," said Macloud sourly, "nobody'd blame *him*. If she hung on, they'd be sorry for him!"

"I'm only taking it into consideration. Certainly there would have to be a very serious reason for murder."

"Well, it wouldn't be because some other girl was jealous, or her parents were jealous for her. Not nowadays."

"Would her people consider Bruce Dunbar ineligible?" Gamadge, his legs stretched out, was smoking thoughtfully.

"Absolutely not," replied Macloud. "They'd have loved it. They'd have staked them. They're very fond of Bruce Dunbar."

"A fortune hunter would have to take the long view."

"I don't know that Bruce Dunbar is a fortune hunter, and there's no evidence that he ever even looked at Alice Dunbar—unless he had to. And she seems to have considered him a lightweight."

"I'm discussing him because she did know him, and she seems to have had some difficulty in meeting men."

Macloud rose, went over to the mantel, and stood knocking out his pipe against the long-suffering bricks of the hearth. He said: "I can't help thinking she must have gone off purposely: a callous thing to do. These people are losing their minds over the uncertainty; I wish I'd never got into this brutal case."

"She may have gone off her head." Gamadge stood up, finished his drink, and put the glass down. "We don't know enough about her to judge, but some things stick out: she was washed out by the sister from infancy, she couldn't hold on to her man, she didn't make friends. Her family probably regarded her as a failure, fit for nothing but to make herself useful; she was young, perhaps she saw no end to it. Don't *they* think she simply made off, Bob?"

"To work or starve?"

"That's so, she wasn't trained to anything. I don't suppose she'd make much of a living at the gift cards and the wastebaskets. They think she didn't go alone?"

"They don't know what to think, Gamadge, and there isn't a policeman or a newspaper that believes they're keeping anything back." As they walked out into the hall, Macloud grumbled: "I must say I thought you'd have a bright idea or so to contribute to the pool; public-spirited amateur like you. Where's all that armchair criminology? You needn't look at me like that, I know you get out of the chair sometimes. Or perhaps you're tired of doing it free. Why don't you turn pro this time? The Dunbars would pay you anything you liked to ask, and you can use my name."

Gamadge pressed the button for the little elevator. He said: "I'd hate to make a fool of myself."

"That's so, there don't seem to be any clues. Except that bus conductor, who *may* have seen her get on his bus somewhere in the lower seventies, but doesn't remember where she got off!"

Gamadge said nothing. The elevator came, Macloud got into it and moodily waved a hand. "Go to it with my blessing," he said, and the elevator sank from sight.

CHAPTER FOUR

The Other One

MONDAY THE FIFTEENTH was one of those days that sometimes surprise city people in August; pleasant and cool, with that strangeness and difference in the air and sunshine that means a season coming to an end. Gamadge dressed in his thinnest grey flannels, had late breakfast, got out his car, and drove up to his subscription library in the seventies. He sometimes said that if he had to die he wouldn't mind dying in the sunny reading-room, comfortably settled in one of the large chairs, with his favourite humorous periodical open on his knee. The librarians assured him he was welcome, no trouble at all, they'd make it right with the board of governors.

This morning he talked for a while with the ladies at the desk, put Clara down for a couple of books, put himself down for one, turned to leave, and came back again.

"By the way," he said, "somebody I know seems to have died while I was in the country. I missed the obituary, and my wife wants the particulars. Could I have back files of the *Times* for—let's see—better make it four weeks."

The papers were laid out for him on the long table in the catalogue room. Pencil in hand, blank slips at his elbow, he studied the Dunbar case and made an occasional note. Time passed, librarians went out to lunch, others came to relieve them. He sat on absorbed until two o'clock.

At last he put his slips in his wallet, got up, and left. He drove around the corner, had lunch, and then got into his car again and headed for the West Side Highway.

He drove up the Henry Hudson Parkway as far as Yonkers, where he cut back to North Broadway; he liked that thoroughfare, with its big trees and its glimpses of the river. He left Hastings behind him, and after another ten minutes slowed down and began to look for road signs. He turned off the route and stopped at the entrance to a small old estate with a shadowy lawn and a circular driveway.

The house, barely visible among the trees, was not far back from the road; he turned in, and drew up in front of a *porte-cochère*. The place seemed to sleep; turreted and gabled, it belonged to the past and seemed rooted there. Faint summer noises came from the gardens and grounds; the scrape of a hoe, the twitter of birds, a rustling as of rabbits in grass.

He got out and rang. Footsteps sounded on bare boards, and the door opened; a thin woman in a dotted silk dress looked out at him.

"You're Miss Cole," Gamadge informed her.

"Yes, sir."

"Staying on to look after the place, I suppose?"

"Yes, sir."

"I'm an associate of Mr. Macloud's, Miss Cole; you know Mr. Macloud? Mr. Dunbar's partner."

"Oh, yes, sir." She swung the door wide. "Come right in."

He followed her through a dim hallway, from which stairs rose. At a double doorway on the right he paused and turned. "That's where Mrs. Woodworth was found, isn't it?"

"Oh, yes, sir. That's where I found her." Her pleasant face showed an old distress. "It was so sad. She must have been coming down for her tea. I didn't hear a thing—I was alone here, you know; it was a Sunday afternoon, and the Russi couple were out."

"I know. Well, at least she didn't fall downstairs."

"They don't know, sir; I hope not. She'd had the other stroke before. I do wish I'd been right there, but I was getting the tray ready in the pantry."

"You could not have done anything for her, Miss Cole."

"I know, but I wish I'd been there."

"These sudden deaths are harder on the bystanders than on the old person who dies."

"I know." She asked: "You didn't come about that, sir?"

"Oh no, I'm just clearing up some details for the estate." He smiled at her. "I should think you'd be sick of us."

"I'm only too glad to do anything I can." She led the way into a dusky high-ceilinged parlour, shuttered against the sun. "I was Mrs. Woodworth's housekeeper for twenty-four years. She's left me comfortable for the rest of my life."

"Yes, I was glad to know it."

"Please sit down, sir." Miss Cole went to a high, narrow window and let in some greenish light, which had to find its way through vines and shrubbery into the room. She said: "And now this other terrible thing."

"Yes, awful." Gamadge waited until she had taken a chair, and then sat opposite her on a hard sofa. He looked around him. "I hope the place won't be torn down. I like these fine old houses."

"It's got to go, sir. The hospital will never keep it. And all McBride's lovely vegetables and flowers and fruit trees."

"They'll be salvaged, I'm sure."

"They belong here," said Miss Cole. "All these years!"

Gamadge nodded in solemn sympathy. The room was solemn, with its bareness and its shrouded furniture, the grand piano in a dark corner, the great bronze clock and flanking urns.

"Have they heard anything about poor Miss Dunbar, sir?"

"Not a thing."

"We just can't understand it. Such a quiet young lady, and just the way she always was at Christmastime, when they were here. And such a handsome card she did for Mrs. Woodworth."

"Yes, it's a mystery. May I smoke, Miss Cole?"

"Of course, sir. There's that bronze ashtray."

"It looks more like a card tray," said Gamadge, pulling it across a little ormulu table towards him.

"Mrs. Woodworth had it for the boys."

"Oh yes, her hospital cases. How's Dobbs?"

"I think he's going on all right; she got him the job. She was always getting things done for people."

"Was he the last, Miss Cole?" Gamadge added: "I know he hasn't been up for a long time. I had a sort of idea that there was another one."

Miss Cole had hesitated, and now looked at him in a puzzled kind of way. "Well, she did have—but he just dropped in."

"Really?" Gamadge spoke with polite interest.

"I mean he..." She looked at him, the puzzled expression growing in her eyes. "How did you hear about him, sir? They never asked me about him, they just took Mrs. Woodworth's address book and got the other names. Such nice boys, they used to be all over the place, fooling with McBride and sometimes driving her in the car. They cheered her up."

"Of course they did. Didn't the other one cheer her up?"

"I guess he did."

"But not you?" Gamadge smiled at her. "Perhaps you didn't care for the idea—strangers dropping in on Mrs. Woodworth?"

"I didn't, and the Russis didn't. McBride didn't. But she seemed to like him."

"Who was he?" Gamadge was lighting a cigarette.

"We don't know."

Gamadge raised his eyes to glance at her over the flame of his lighter. She went on: "Mrs. Woodworth didn't say. Of course there's no reason why she should. She just told us the first time—after he came the first time—that he was driving by, and saw the place, and walked in to look at it because he was a landscape gardener."

"Walked in?" Gamadge replaced his lighter in his pocket.

"He left his car in the road every time," said Miss Cole.

"Perhaps he wasn't proud of it."

"It must have been some rattletrap kind of thing."

"Oh."

"I suppose he was a gentleman," said Miss Cole, rather grimly, "or Mrs. Woodworth wouldn't have had him."

"War hero, perhaps," suggested Gamadge.

Miss Cole's smile was sardonic. "He was older than the boys; over thirty anyway. And I hate those flashy sport clothes. Russi said that first time he brought in the tea—"'What does Madam want with that gigolo?'"

"I see. Might be an artistic type, Miss Cole; landscape gardening is certainly an art."

"He never went near the gardens after that first day, when he walked around with Mrs. Woodworth. He wasn't here much," she added. "He only started coming last September, and he hasn't been near the place since June. He'd come about once in two months, have his tea and go."

"What *did* Mrs. Woodworth see in him, I wonder?"

"Well, he'd sing."

"Sing? Was he a professional?"

"I don't know, sir. He'd— "She turned and looked at the great dark bulk of the closed piano. "He'd play and sing sometimes, that's all. You'd hear him all over the house, way back in the kitchen; and I must say you could have cried sometimes."

"Sad music? Crooning?"

"No, just songs, beautiful. There was one—the only time I ever heard words: 'Don't Fill Up a Glass for Me'."

Gamadge laughed. "I could cry over that song any time; the harmonies are wonderful. I could cry over it cold sober."

Miss Cole smiled too. "I wouldn't blame you, sir."

Gamadge crossed his knees. "What did he look like, this accomplished party?"

"You could hardly see him. It's always so dim in here, and in winter Mrs. Woodworth only liked soft light; and he never looked at *us*."

"Didn't he?"

"Mrs. Russi never saw him at all; McBride only saw him way off across the orchard. Russi and I—we weren't supposed to stare at visitors when we brought in a tray, and I only brought the tray on Sundays."

"You must have got an impression. The whole thing's so odd—you've really got me very much interested in the landscape gardener."

"Brown hair, glasses, quite good-looking, a heavy tan."

"Even in winter?"

"He may have had a naturally dark skin, I suppose. It looked more like tan."

"And then these loud clothes."

"Coat with big checks; and a terrible necktie."

"Even in winter?"

"Yes, sir."

Gamadge rose and went over to the piano; he looked through the music in the canterbury, the books of songs, shook his head. "No Stephen Foster here. He must have known it by heart."

"What, sir?" She had turned in her chair to watch him.

"'Comrades, Fill No Glass for Me'; what he sang." Gamadge came back and sat down again. "I wonder what he was after."

Miss Cole was frightened. "There's nothing missing."

"No, of course not. I mean, why should this raffish young man drive all the way from—anywhere, to call on an old lady?"

"We thought he wanted the job of doing the grounds up, sir."

"But McBride was never consulted?"

"Not a word was said." She added anxiously: "I hope there's nothing wrong?"

"Not a thing, so far as I know."

"Mrs. Woodworth wasn't an old lady that talked much about her affairs to anybody. She had a horror of being interfered with, sir; she was always afraid that the family would want to take her affairs out of her hands. She didn't want them told that she had that first stroke, only the doctor insisted."

"I understand."

"We understood her, sir. The family was afraid we—just the servants, you know—couldn't take proper care of her. But they didn't blame us because she died that way, all alone."

"Naturally not. It's the most difficult thing in the world, making suitable arrangements for old people and keeping them happy about it."

"So we never talked about her to the family."

"Or about her guests."

"No, sir."

"Especially since she wasn't too fond of her relations?"

"She thought very highly of Mr. Dunbar's business ability," said Miss Cole. "But Mrs. Dunbar was very interfering. That poor Miss Dunbar, what could have become of her? I wouldn't think anything could."

"Become of her?" Gamadge asked it drily. "Hardly anything, one would say."

"I mean happen to her."

"It's very ironical—if anything did." Gamadge rose. "I suppose the police didn't bother you much up here after she disappeared. But they must have inquired here, as everywhere."

"They did," said Miss Cole, getting up. "I never could see why. It isn't as if she ever came alone to see Mrs. Woodworth."

"If she wandered off, temporarily out of her mind, she might go anywhere she'd ever been before."

Miss Cole said, looking rather white: "They were all over the place, sir."

"That's routine, Miss Cole." He moved out into the hall. "You're quite comfortable here? Not nervous at night?"

"Oh no, sir, I have the burglar alarm; and McBride is right out there in his room over the garage—it's only a step away. And the garage is wired too. Mrs. Woodworth was afraid of getting a car stolen. It's lonely here, you know."

"Well, I'll just wander around the premises, and report all in order to Macloud. And thank you very much."

"It's nice of them to send up."

Gamadge went out into the cool of the *porte-cochère*, down the steps, and around the house. There were masses of shrubbery, formal flowerbeds and borders, gravelled paths. The old carriage house, gabled and turreted to match the Woodworth residence, was just across the driveway in the rear; now a garage and workshop, gardener's quarters and toolshed, its upper windows commanded a view of all the cultivated ground, vegetable plots as well as flower plots. They would be within earshot, too, unless McBride happened to be stone deaf.

Behind the garage stretched an orchard, then a stubble-field; beyond that barbed wire cut off the next estate. Alice Dunbar was not here; the police would have been over every foot of orchard and meadow for signs of digging, and nobody could dig unheard, even in the dead of night, nearer the house.

He walked back to his car, and found a little gnarled old man beside it, looking at it with reserved approbation. As Gamadge approached he squinted up at him and put a finger to the brim of his hat.

Gamadge nodded. "Mr. McBride?"

Mr. McBride was far from deaf, and it seemed that he had been in communication with Miss Cole. He said: "I'm McBride. And there's no news of the young leddy."

"No, none at all."

McBride muttered something to the effect that it wasn't canny.

Gamadge wagged his head. "And I know what you're thinking, you old image," he told himself "It isn't canny because Alice Dunbar wasn't bonny. If she'd been bonny, or even soncy, whatever happened to her would be canny enough, no matter how horrible." Looking around him, he said: "You've kept this place up wonderfully. I don't know why the Aaron Means doesn't keep it on as a convalescent home."

"I don't know mysel'."

"Macloud ought to put it up to Mr. Dunbar."

The image—he really did look as if he had been hacked out of hardwood—approved of this to the surprising extent of opening the car door, waiting while Gamadge got in, and closing it after him. Finger to hat-brim, he watched the convertible depart.

The August light was mellowing and failing. Gamadge bitterly reflected how much time and trouble it took, this not making a fool of one's self. If he had been willing to ask a few questions of Macloud, he needn't have spent all those hours in the library, looking up names and addresses and verifying his data. But nobody could get much farther in this case, or so it seemed, by working in the open; and Macloud wouldn't be able to back him if he worked out of line.

It was obvious that nobody in authority had connected those two happenings—Alice Dunbar's disappearance and Mrs. Ames Woodworth's death. Gamadge hadn't exactly connected them, he had merely toyed with the idea; and it led to the further idea that Alice Dunbar—who knew so few and such unlikely men—might possibly have known a man through her great-aunt Woodworth. A protégé? Hardly the protégés that Gamadge had already heard of; someone else?

The other one had materialized, and Gamadge felt free to indulge his imagination.

He imagined a sensational little drama: a mysterious stranger arriving, introducing himself, ingratiating himself, making himself familiar with household procedure in the afternoon. He could certainly get an impression of the front-door key, or perhaps he took note of that dining-room window that Gamadge had seen standing open; a french window, masked in shrubbery, across the house from the parlour.

He might have come a little early one Sunday afternoon, when the Russi couple would be out and McBride not working; he would know by this time that Mrs. Woodworth took a nap until teatime. He would go softly up the stairs; wait in the shadows until the old lady came out of her room and began to descend…

"Everything there except his motive," reflected Gamage, dropped his motive as at present unguessable, and went on to sum up against the landscape gardener, old Mrs. Woodworth's raffish friend:

He always left his car in the road, an odd thing to do, at least in the winter months. A sensible thing to do, if he didn't want his licence plate read. An imperative necessity on the day of his last visit to the Woodworth place.

He never looked a servant in the face. Safe enough to look at his hostess, who wouldn't be on hand to testify against him if he brought the murder off but failed to cover his tracks.

His appearance suggested disguise. Part of the disguise might have been the mannerism that caused Russi to describe him as a gigolo. The all-the-year-round tan, the glasses, the loud clothes and the frightful cravat—not such bad camouflage for a pale young man who normally dressed as neutrally as Gamadge himself did, and whose sight was perfect.

Gamadge, paying his toll on the West Side Highway, was worrying about the young man's motive again; for without it he couldn't get anywhere.

CHAPTER FIVE

Comment

WHILE HIS FAMILY was away Gamadge often dined out, to make things easier for his staff of one. Today he had given Theodore the afternoon and evening off, and so when he reached home the house was empty.

Too empty. As soon as he got inside the front door the emptiness hit him in the face. He turned into his office, picked up the telephone, and asked for long distance. When he heard Clara's breathless voice—she must have been running, could it be possible that in the turmoil of the summer cottage she had felt a solitude too?—he spoke in the flat tone of desolation:

"You're still alive."

"And so are you!"

"That's out of the way, then." Returning briskly to normal, he said: "I may not be out this week after all."

"Oh how ghastly."

"Aren't you living a full, rich life, my darling?"

"Very. The doggy chases all the bicycles, and the kitty has run away."

"Get the kitty back," said Gamadge, sincerely disturbed by this news.

"He'll be back for supper. He can never catch anything."

"The cat's incompetent. He ought to have his affairs taken out of his paws and administered." Gamadge added: "You say nothing about the boy, Mrs. Squeers; bobbish, I hope?"

"That's the word."

"Oh, by the way, Clara; didn't you say while I was up there, the last week in July it was, that you knew a certain lady who was in the papers at the time and still is? I mean the parent, you know."

"Why so cryptic?"

"Because we might get in the papers ourselves if I wasn't; everybody's so agog about it."

"I didn't say I knew her, Henry. I thought I did, but I don't. I mean I met her five or six times, and I sat next to her at lunch and at a tea; but the last time I saw her she cut me in an elevator."

"Oh? Why?"

"Well, I bowed first."

"Clara, I didn't think you were the sort to push yourself forward like that. What got into you?"

"I just thought she'd forgotten her glasses."

"What's she like when she isn't frightened by ill-bred people like you?"

"Oh, quite pleasant and gossipy; quite an agreeable old b—brute."

"Watch it," said Gamadge, who was laughing helplessly. "I think there's some kind of a law."

"We oughtn't to be laughing at her now."

"That's so; I can't help feeling that they don't treat their lame ducks very well in that family, though. What would you say?"

"I don't know. They'd have to behave awfully to have a thing like this happen, wouldn't they? I mean if she—"

"Careful." Gamadge changed the conversation. At the end of it he went upstairs and put his light flannels and his Panama away; he would not be wearing them for some time.

He changed to dark-brown worsteds, garaged his car, and walked down to a club where he would be sure to see some old classmates.

He found one or two at the bar, and he was not much surprised to find Arthur Jennings among them. Jennings lived with his mother; while she was in the country he patronized the club, looking for companionship to other stranded alumni. He was a long-chinned man, solemn and earnest; even wallflowers at dances shrank when they saw him coming, and said they had twisted their ankles and would rather sit this one out, please.

Everybody was talking about the Dunbar case, which was not surprising either. It was still a mainstay of conversation to rich and poor. Gamadge, who cherished the workings of the human mind when it occupied itself with rumour, listened quietly.

He heard that the police knew exactly where Alice Dunbar was; she was in a sanatorium in French Lick, had taken dope for years.

No, that wasn't right, the trouble was alcoholism and she was in a hospital in Cheyenne.

Nothing of the kind. The family knew exactly where she was; right here in New York, out of her head; it ran in the family on the mother's side.

Somebody had had an airmail letter from Paris; this was a fact, a schoolmate had seen her in Paris in a black-and-white dress, talking to a man with a beard and a green hat.

Gamadge couldn't help asking if there was snow on the hat; but as he seemed to be the only man at the bar who remembered tales of the other war, he got blank looks from his neighbours and nothing more.

Rumour gave way to conjecture. A little rosy-faced man whom Gamadge didn't know said he didn't blame her a bit if she skipped out. "I only knew her slightly, years ago, but Abigail walked all over her. It would have been all right if the engagement had stuck, but after that fell through..." He shook his head.

Jennings, bristling a little, said that the Dunbar family was a united family and a happy one. "Old Mrs. Dunbar is charming, a delightful woman."

"Oh, very," said the rosy-faced man, "when you're giving her twenty dollars for a ticket for one of those damned benefits."

"She is tireless when it comes to her charities, even now. She's not at all well," said Jennings stiffly.

"I should think she'd be dead," said somebody else. "Toughest thing I ever heard of. You know why that engagement was broken, Elkins?"

The rosy man knew, of course. "He fell in love with the other girl, girl from his hometown. Alice had a nervous breakdown and they took her to Hot Springs."

"You don't know that," protested Jennings.

"Everybody knows it."

Gamadge had now recognized the third man as somebody named Wyn. He nodded, and Wyn turned to him:

"Hello, Gamadge, aren't you a friend of Macloud's—the Dunbar partner?"

"I am, yes," said Gamadge, who had ordered an old-fashioned and was sipping it slowly.

"What does *he* say? What's the lowdown? Don't they really know where she is?"

"He says they don't."

"Any ideas on the subject?"

"I'm getting them now," said Gamadge, and smiled. "From what I hear, she ought to have left years ago."

"That's right. After the broken engagement the family never did a thing for her. No dinners, nothing; so of course she more or less dropped out of things."

Jennings spoke up again with obstinate loyalty: "Mrs. Dunbar has been ill with blood pressure for ages; of course they can't entertain." He added gloomily: "And this will finish them forever."

"It hasn't finished Gail Tanner," said somebody at the other end of the bar. "She's going around to quiet bars of an evening, just like always. Saw her at one the other afternoon with a very handsome guy."

Jennings said angrily: "She feels all this deeply. Deeply. Trying to get a little diversion now and then—that isn't going *out*. She's living very quietly at the Stanton. I was there the other night."

"Well, sorry," said the unknown, and Gamadge leaned forward to placate the Dunbars' champion:

"They don't mean anything, Artie; you might be gibbering away like this yourself if you didn't know the people. They wouldn't talk in this strain if they thought Alice Dunbar was dead."

"Dead? Dead?" Little Elkins was shocked. "What do you mean, dead? Nobody ever thought she was dead. She just took it on the lam."

"With some man the family wouldn't have let her marry," added the unknown. "So there wouldn't be an unholy row."

"You wouldn't call this an unholy row?" asked Gamadge.

"I mean, they can't get after the man and make things hot for him."

"She's of age."

"And then some. But they could make things hot; you don't know old Dunbar."

"What could he do?"

"What couldn't he do, with his money and connections, to some nobody?"

"But there's no money involved, is there? The nobody can't swindle them out of anything."

Jennings finished his drink, said coldly that Mr. Angus Dunbar was a man of the highest principles, professional and moral, signed his cheque, and stalked away. Gamadge, watching him go, asked himself why, in spite of length and boniness, he gave the impression of being not a thin man but a thick one. He decided that it was because Artie walked leaning backward, with his stomach always slightly in advance of him.

Elkins had been watching him also. He said: "Poor old man, he's having the time of his life, propping up the Dunbars."

The unknown tossed off his cocktail. "Wonder why Abigail Tanner is letting him hang around. He can't prop *her* up."

"Well, she wouldn't be going around much now, sitting in a bar now and then doesn't count," said Elkins. "And she can't stand being alone a minute. Jennings is alive, you have to give him that."

"I hope he doesn't think he'll finally make the grade there," said the unknown. "Boy! You should have seen what she had in tow the other afternoon. Looked like an actor."

He went off. Gamadge followed him into the dining-room, sat in the corner farthest away from Jennings, and read a newspaper until his lobster came. He wrenched his mind away from the indigestible Dunbar case, or tried to; but it persisted in travelling along routes that were hardly less upsetting. People falling off bicycles to the sound of loud barking; lawsuits and damages; a yellow cat starving in the woods, or marooned up some tall tree; a little boy vainly calling to it along the roads. Clara always minimized her troubles—was she being interviewed by constables, the sheriff, state police?

"If I got up early for once in my life," he thought, "I could finish my own job tomorrow and drive up to the cottage on Wednesday. And what's keeping me here?"

Probably nothing more, he reflected with disgust, than an impecunious fellow in a precarious profession, drumming up trade; riding around in such a rattletrap of a car that he didn't like to park it under *porte-cochères*. A fellow who owned but one suit, and cultivated that bogus tan under sunlamps to go with the sports clothes he had to wear. If he didn't look at servants, perhaps they weren't much to look at. The old lady had played him along for the sake of being entertained and having a man in the house. It wouldn't be the first time that a wealthy patron had encouraged an artist and then dropped him.

Gamadge had his lobster and his coffee, and walked home. In the library he got out his notes again, and went through them—he assured himself—for the last time. Midway down a scrawled slip he paused, reread it, sat studying it with his elbows on the desk and his hands in his hair.

Theodore appeared silently, arranged the whisky, ice, and tumbler on a little table, brought the table close. Gamadge said: "Thanks. Enjoy yourself?"

"I did, sir."

He departed. Gamadge sat back in his chair, mixed himself a drink, lighted a cigarette. "Macloud told me all that; but I..." He smoked, his eyes on the cornice. He'd have a shot at it, no harm in that. After all, it was pretty late in the summer; there was a good chance, and here was the telephone book.

CHAPTER SIX

The Private Life

NEXT MORNING GAMADGE dressed himself in his last change of summer wear—an Oxford mixture with an unlined coat, the last relic of his English clothes, and much cherished by him. He walked across to Fifth Avenue, down Fifth, and around into Fifty-seventh Street.

He stopped in front of a narrow old building on the north side of the block, with an art shop on the ground floor and other business premises all the way to the roof. He craned back to see the small gilt sign painted on one of the top windows—*Bransome. Paintings.*

An open door beside the entrance to the art shop led into a dingy little hallway with torn linoleum underfoot and steam pipes running up to a metal ceiling. The elevator at the end of the passage had a folding gate, and a sign over the push-button said: *Bell out of Order.*

He rattled the gate, and the elevator creaked into sight from depths below. A bald old man shoved the gate back.

"Miss Bransome."

They shuddered upwards, stopping at every floor to look for stranded passengers. When Gamadge got out, he asked: "Can you hear the gate rattle from this landing?"

"Sure can."

"Thanks."

There were only two doors on the landing, one at the front and one at the rear. The rear door stood open, and he stepped into a narrow hallway; its woodwork was painted green and its walls were papered with a copy of an old-fashioned design—birds on trellises. The south end of the passage led into what looked like a sitting-room; the north end into a studio.

He walked diffidently to the studio doorway; unframed pictures stood on the ground facing the wall, studies and watercolour sketches were pinned up everywhere, there was a lopsided dummy in a corner, and an easel with an unfinished picture on it was placed to get the north light. The picture was a watercolour of an apple and grapes.

A little woman in a green smock sat working at a long table to the right of the door. She saw Gamadge, and rose. Gamadge said: "So glad to find you in town, Miss Bransome; but I don't suppose you share my satisfaction. Was it nice up in Vermont?"

She was a thin little woman with dark eyes and dark untidy hair. The eyes surveyed him from behind pince-nez. She said: "My sketching class only runs through July."

"So I thought when I decided to look you up."

Miss Bransome slowly took him in. She asked very doubtfully: "Would you be the owner? I told the agent, I told him distinctly, that I would give up the front room before I'd pay any more rent."

A New Englander. Gamadge said: "Don't blame you. I'm not the owner, Miss Bransome."

"I didn't suppose so." Her eyes seemed to inquire: "*Could* you be an art patron at this time of the year? Or the parent of a new pupil?" But she left it to Gamadge to explain:

"I just wanted a little information." Finding it even more difficult to go on than he had expected, he crossed over to the easel: "That's a nice study."

Miss Bransome smiled faintly, glancing at the disintegrated remains of the study, which now lay on a plate—apple peelings and grape skins. She said: "I ate it for lunch. Hope I'll get more like it tomorrow."

Gamadge said: "Now if the portrait painters could only eat the sitters!"

"I guess they'd like to, sometimes."

The thing wasn't getting easier, it was getting harder. Gamadge turned to face her. "I'm not an official of any sort, Miss Bransome; just doing some confidential work, more or less at my own discretion. Would you tell me where Alice Dunbar used to go when she was supposed to be here painting?"

Miss Bransome backed up against the work-table and gripped the edge of it with both hands. Her eyes were fastened on his, her face had turned ash-colour.

He said: "You might not have to come into it."

"How did you—" Her voice broke.

"Just to make you feel better about it, I'll tell you—if you'll sit down."

She sank into the hard chair, nicely painted and decorated, that she had been sitting in before. "I've been sick about it," she said in a whisper.

"I can imagine." Gamadge pulled another of the painted chairs up to face her, sat down, and got out his cigarettes. "You smoke, Miss Bransome?"

She shook her head, still gazing at him.

"May I?"

She put her arm out blindly, and got her fingers on a green pottery bowl. Gamadge rose to take it from her, put it on a stool beside him, and lighted a cigarette.

"Nobody asked me," whispered Miss Bransome.

"They only asked whether you'd heard from her after she disappeared?"

She nodded. "I know I should have—but how could I tell whether it would help, and the Dunbars—and I'd be in the papers and they might not have believed I didn't know anything."

"But you did, didn't you?"

"She told me it was this nice young couple, artists; her mother and father wouldn't have cared for them, they'd have asked a lot of questions about who they were and where they came from and silly stuff like that. They were just nice young people from the West, with no money. Alice wanted friends of her own." Miss Bransome was speaking fast, almost angrily. "And she hasn't been near them since last spring."

"When did she start going?"

"Last fall, October. She didn't go every week, only about once a month. I don't believe they have a thing to do with it, not a thing!"

Gamadge dropped ash in the pottery bowl. Leaning forward to do so, not looking at her, he asked: "How did she happen to meet them? Did she say?"

"Of course she said! Naturally I asked her, when she first wanted me to—wanted me to—" Miss Bransome couldn't find the word. She paused, and at last ended faintly: "Help her."

"What did she tell you?" Gamadge sat back again.

"It was really an accident, and they were so nice about it. Some friends were driving her home from a theatre party—"

"I thought she was always carted around in the family car."

"Yes, but these were people who had a car, and they often brought her home. But this time she found they had an appointment way downtown, and they'd be late, so she insisted on taking a cab part of the way. And there was this nice store right on the avenue, with soda and fruit. She was thirsty. She went in and had the soda, and then she found she had no money! She hardly ever needed it, you know. And these nice young people were there, sitting beside her at the counter, and she was so terribly mortified, and they lent her the change."

"It's a friendly town," commented Gamadge, "especially to people like Alice Dunbar."

"Yes, but she was mortified. Of course she wanted to pay them back and thank them, and they'd given her their address and asked her to come. Where was the harm? She was a grown woman. I've been going around by myself since I was a child. I've been teaching since I was eighteen." Miss Bransome snatched a checked handkerchief out of her pocket, covered her face with it, and began to cry.

Gamadge said: "Don't cry, Miss Bransome. You're upset because you didn't believe a word of that story."

She sobbed, and Gamadge caught disconnected phrases: "No life of her own…wasn't appreciated…grown woman…"

"I know; you were sorry for her."

She looked up. "I knew her when she was at school, I used to come to the house to give her lessons when she'd been sick. All she had was her painting." Miss Bransome glanced at a cupboard behind the work-table. "Beautiful work, people don't realize how much work and study goes into illumination and lettering. You don't know—" She sobbed again. "All I've been through since she left! She might have told me."

"And you haven't a clue to these people? To where she went when she—er—wasn't here?"

Miss Bransome said slowly: "If they were nice, and they didn't have anything to do with it and don't know where she is, I'd hate to drag them into it. Young people like that—it might hurt them. I mean not coming forward and saying anything. Like me."

"Wouldn't hurt them at all. They weren't in your position, Miss Bransome."

Tears again filled her eyes. "You couldn't say I was in a position of responsibility. I did take the money for the lessons, because I was giving her the time, even if she wasn't here. And it was her money, she paid me out of her own allowance. And she wasn't the flighty type. But I did feel—one day I followed her."

"Sensible."

"I did feel a responsibility, I just couldn't help feeling one. I mean she never did give me their name or their address."

"That told you something."

"I couldn't *believe*—"

"Would you have blamed her? If her family was so very fastidious?" Gamadge smiled at her.

Miss Bransome said: "You don't know them. When her engagement was broken they weren't kind at all. They have no feelings!" She spoke with considerable violence. "When I went there to give her a lesson, I had my lunch on a tray!"

Gamadge looked grave and shook his head.

"It's not far from here," said Miss Bransome. "She could walk it in a few minutes. And there *is* a couple on the top floor. I asked in the basement."

"Superintendent?"

"No, she doesn't come in the afternoon. There's a store in the basement."

"You'd give me this address?"

Searching his face anxiously, she asked: "Did you say you don't have to tell?"

"Not if it isn't necessary."

"But how did you know? If you know, you must have heard about me somewhere."

"I might have guessed."

"Guessed?"

"Well, you seemed to be her only chance, Miss Bransome. I mean you were the only person she seems to have been alone with at regular intervals, over a long period of time. The lessons were two hours long; you can go places in two hours."

She said in a low voice, looking down at her hands, "If it hadn't been a nice kind of little apartment house, and there hadn't been a couple there, I'd have spoken to her."

"Of course."

"If I'd said anything, after she left, the Dunbars—I'd rather have died."

"Difficult. One gets into these things, and it isn't so easy to explain."

"And she hadn't been going there for so long."

"That's your out, of course."

She got up, went out of the room, and came back after a minute or two with a scrap of paper. Rising, he took it from her. As he looked down at her, at the small pale face so full of pride and self-respect and anxiety, he could not help smiling at the thought of those lunches on a tray. She had got even with the Dunbars.

He expressed something of this when he said: "They're having a bad time, you know—the Dunbar family. Their worst enemy couldn't wish them a rougher time."

She was not to be softened. "I wish you knew them! And I wish I'd been there to see their faces when they found out they weren't getting that Woodworth money."

It was Gamadge's turn to back up against the table. The idea was not entirely a surprising one to him, it had occurred to him before; but her definite confirmation of it was something of a shock. He asked after a moment: "Did they expect it?"

"Of course they did. For Alice. They thought it was coming to her after the aunt died. I'm sorry *she* didn't get it. She was to have it because Abigail had Richfield Tanner's."

"You mean it was settled? In a will?"

"They thought so! I always say, wait till the party dies. When I saw that will in the papers, I actually laughed. That old lady was leaving it to that hospital all the time! Of course *they* have plenty; Alice would always have been comfortable. Oh, what *has* become of her?"

"Alice Dunbar told you in so many words that she was getting the Woodworth fortune?"

Miss Bransome was irritated by his slowness of comprehension. "Fifty times!"

"Well."

She followed him out to the landing. "I just can't tell you how thankful I'll be if you'll keep my name out of this. I might not get another pupil as long as I lived."

Gamadge said rather drily that he understood that.

"Some of them are young, you know; just children. It was different with Alice Dunbar, but parents mightn't understand."

"Try not to worry, Miss Bransome. I'll do my best and I'll call you."

"Oh, will you? Oh, thank you so much. There's one thing," she said, crumpling the smock in a pathetic hand, "she never mentioned me."

"To the nice young couple?"

"Whoever they were."

"I can see that she'd be mortified at having to confess what shifts she was put to to see a friend."

"And she wouldn't give me away."

Gamadge rattled the gate of the elevator. He said: "This thing, such as it is—do you have it at night?"

"Indeed I don't; it goes off at six in winter, five in summer. Twelve on Saturdays."

"Lots of stairs for a tenant."

"Well, I'm the only one that sleeps in the place, and I'm so tired at night I stay home."

CHAPTER SEVEN

Nice Couple

GAMADGE WALKED DOWN the avenue, and then a good way east. When he turned in to the block he wanted, he saw why Miss Bransome had not described it; it was not nice at all. It was dreary and gritty, very grey under the now overcast sky. Small wholesale supply stores—plumbers, upholsterers, surgical appliances—occupied the basements and first floor fronts; this would not be a shopping centre for Dunbars or their friends. Alice Dunbar might safely visit here, especially in the afternoons, when superintendents were away and the business people back at their work.

The house he wanted was nice enough, however; a stucco-fronted walk-up with a stationers' supply store in the basement, a printing plant above it, a firm of architects above that. The third-storey windows were shuttered, the top apartment had neat curtains of watermelon pink. The nice couple was in residence.

Gamadge mounted steps of pierced ironwork to the clean vestibule. A typed card beside the top bell said *Steadman*; under it a fading pencil scrawl had been crossed out, but he deciphered the name—*Fuller.* He pushed the Steadmans' bell, opened the door when the lock clicked, and climbed the stairs.

A girl stood waiting for him on the last landing, in front of an open doorway. She was a very pretty girl, with clear features and candid blue eyes; her bronze hair curled on her neck, and she wore a print dress of expensive quality and cut. She smiled, the smile of one who has always had the goodwill of her fellow mortals.

Gamadge asked: "Fuller?"

"Oh, I'm sorry, you pushed the wrong bell. And I'm afraid Mr. Fuller has gone."

"I'm awfully sorry I disturbed you. I had an idea there was a vacancy here, and there doesn't seem to be a superintendent on the premises."

"Mrs. Flynn is only here from twelve to two, and it isn't quite twelve yet. Would you"—the candid eyes had candidly taken Gamadge in—"care to wait?"

"That's much too kind."

A large, fair young man was working at a drawing board in the room behind her. He now looked around, rose, and came to the door. He was wearing a shirt that had certainly been part of his flying outfit; collar open, sleeves rolled high. He said: "Come on in, it's a hellish climb."

"Mighty nice of you, if I won't be in the way."

"You think I want an excuse to knock off work?"

They all laughed, and Gamadge followed Mrs. Steadman into a pleasant room with chintz cushions on the wicker furniture, a very fine old French rug on the floorboards, and a framed oil of flowers over the mantel. It had no doubt been the servants' room once, when the house had been a private residence; but its little open fireplace and grey-marble chimney piece would put the rent up nowadays.

Hot up here under the roof, although there was a free current of air through open doors to the back windows; and young Steadman, looming huge under the rather low-pitched ceiling, must feel the heat; but he looked satisfied with life.

"Sit down," he said. His wife had already settled herself on a couch, and Gamadge sat near her. Steadman resumed his place in front of his drawing board, turning his chair to face them. Gamadge looked with polite interest at the blueprint.

"I work for an architect," said Steadman, "downtown. I don't do anything at home as a rule, but this is part of my vacation. I came home from the beach to put in some licks on a competition I went in for."

Mrs. Steadman said: "I hope you will move in, if Mr. Fuller's really gone for good. I'm alone in the house so much. Jim doesn't like it, but I don't mind."

"Fuller was a rock, was he?" Gamadge had refused young Steadman's offer of a cigarette, and was lighting one of his own.

Steadman laughed. "We never laid eyes on him."

"That's New York for you."

"We only moved in ourselves in June," said Mrs. Steadman. "The families thought we were crazy, but we go up to stay with them—Jim's or mine—every weekend, and it's rather fun in the city. And we had to take the flat then, or probably never."

Gamadge, looking around him, said they were lucky. Nice place.

"Fuller's is bigger and of course cooler," said Steadman. "And a damn sight more money. It was Scale's, you know."

"Scale's?"

"He's the owner; old boy owns the house. I thought sure you'd have a personal pull with him; they say he never rents to anybody he doesn't personally know about."

"He knows my family," said Mrs. Steadman.

"I haven't a prayer," said Gamadge. "I just dropped in. Somebody said there might be a flat."

"Hope you get it," said Steadman, looking him over.

"Thanks. I'm sorry Mr. Scale is so particular."

"You know us." Mrs. Steadman laughed.

"By Jove I do!"

"Ought to be easy enough to dig up a reference," said Steadman. "Reason the old geezer is so fussy, the flat's full of his furniture and stuff. They used to live here—his family—

from way back; then they lost money, and they all died but Scale, so he kept the third floor and rented the rest."

"The superintendent was an old servant in the family," said Mrs. Steadman. "She does all the renting for him. There isn't much work here for her, with all the business firms downstairs. They take care of their own places, and there's an oil furnace. She's such a nice woman."

"I see it's feudal," said Gamadge. "So Mr. Fuller was only a sort of sublet?"

"That's so," said Steadman. He looked at his wife. "Probably moving out so Scale can move back."

Mrs. Steadman shook her head. "No, Jimmie, Mr. Scale isn't coming back until Thanksgiving. He never does."

"I wouldn't want a place for three months," said Gamadge.

"Lots of people do," urged Steadman.

"Sometimes Mr. Scale goes right down to Asheville from Canada," said Mrs. Steadman hopefully. "He did last fall, and Mr. Fuller came."

Gamadge asked: "Where did you take your vacation? I'm debating places; haven't had mine yet."

"The first part with my folks," said Steadman, "in the Adirondacks. That was the last two weeks in July. They let me take a third week with her folks in Maine, but as I said I cut it short after all and came back Monday on account of the competition."

"Mountains in July, August the sea," said Gamadge. "You can't beat that schedule." He leaned back, relaxed and cheerful. "Quiet here, is it?"

"Well, we have a night club in the rear," said Mrs. Steadman.

"I'll say we have," agreed Steadman. "But we won't get much of the band music when the windows shut down. When we win a competition we'll go there ourselves, be part of the row."

"Every night," declared Mrs. Steadman.

"Another thing," said Steadman. "If you get Fuller's apartment, you get the use of the garden. It goes with the flat."

"No! That's nice," said Gamadge.

"Mr. Scale has his breakfast there when he's at home in summer," said Mrs. Steadman, "and his coffee at night."

"I'll certainly do the same."

"Like to have a look?" Steadman rose. "You'll see that it isn't as public as most yards."

"Very glad to see it."

"And you'll get an idea of the lay-out of the Fuller flat, too. It's like this, only bigger, as I said."

They all moved towards the connecting passage between front and rear; Steadman leading, Gamadge following with Mrs. Steadman. She said: "Don't be shocked at its being so old-fashioned. I'm afraid Mr. Scale doesn't spend much on his tenants. But there's one thing, Mrs. Flynn says he never raises the rent."

"Let the ceilings fall."

"He does necessary repairs," said Mrs. Steadman seriously, "and Mrs. Flynn is awfully nice about what's necessary."

The little kitchen at one side of the passage was so thickly covered with yellow paint that its look of yesterday was quaint rather than mean. The bathroom opposite, from the glimpse Gamadge had of it, seemed cramped for one of Steadman's build, and the old clawfoot tub strangely narrow and high. But the bedroom was delightful, all green and white, with window seats and awnings. Steadman made room for him at a window.

The night club was to the left, its back windows closely barred and latticed; next to it, behind the Scale premises, was the bare brick of a warehouse, next to that something that must be the rear end of a garage. Along the block to the right the houses seemed given up to business—there were plaster statuettes in one window, glassware in another, blank uncurtained oblongs of dusty pane above.

"Yes, you'd be quite private here," said Gamadge, leaning out to look down.

The yard was enclosed by the usual high fence, painted green; there were bushes almost as high as the fence, a tree, flagged paths around the middle plot. This had been bordered with a wide margin of blooming flowers.

"How very nice," said Gamadge.

"It was all turf," explained Mrs. Steadman, leaning out beside him, "but Mr. Fuller had them put the flowers in. Don't you love double petunias?"

"I do."

"The old turf in the middle ought to be replaced; but I suppose he couldn't face that, and now he's gone and can't enjoy the flowers."

"He had them all summer, I suppose."

"Put them in while we were away," said Steadman. "We found them there when we got back. They'll look like the devil if nobody takes care of them. Mrs. Flynn can't do much in the time she's here."

"I'd take care of them if they'd let me," said Mrs. Steadman, "but we're not supposed to go near the garden."

"If I get the flat you can live in it if you want to," said Gamadge.

"And we might put in other flowers!"

"I don't think I'm as rich as Fuller was."

"Oh dear, I keep forgetting how much things cost in the city."

"Shouldn't think you'd need much reminding," said Steadman, gathering her fan of hair into a large brown hand and affectionately pulling it.

Gamadge withdrew his head. "It's a nice outlook. Why on earth did the other people go? I mean the ones that had this flat before you did?"

"They were two ladies, cousins of Mr. Scale," said Mrs. Steadman. "One of them taught in a school, the other just lived with her and kept house. They got too old for the extra stairs."

"When we get too old to climb," said Steadman, "we'd better be rich like Fuller."

"Mrs. Flynn won't have to do any watering today, anyhow." Gamadge craned out again to look at the sky. "It's going to rain sometime. Which reminds me, I ought to go down and see her. Wish me luck."

He pulled back his head again, and they all shook hands. The Steadmans saw him to the top of the stairs. Just like New York, you meet people and even like them, and you don't even know their name; not if you're as polite as the nice couple on the top floor of the Scale house.

CHAPTER EIGHT

References

GAMADGE WENT DOWN the three flights of stairs and out into the vestibule. He pushed the superintendent's bell; Alice Dunbar had stood here, once at least, and pushed a bell—whose?

Not the Steadmans'—they had only moved in last June. Not, presumably, the printer's, or the architect's, or that of the two elderly ladies on the top floor—the "couple" of poor Miss Bransome's information. Alice Dunbar would hardly need to resort to deception in dealing with those.

Mr. Fuller, the tenant who had a personal recommendation, who spent money on flowers but didn't mind the ragged grass of a city backyard? Puzzled and morose, Gamadge waited; but when the door opened he greeted the stout woman in front of him with a smile.

"You're the superintendent?"

"Yes, sir." She was getting on in years, but her colour was still fresh and high and there was hardly any grey in her dark, neatly coiled hair. She looked strong, competent, and amiable. The Scale cook-housekeeper once, perhaps; and she didn't mind coming to the door with a large clean apron over her black-and-white print dress.

"I had some kind of an idea, Mrs. Flynn, that the Fuller apartment was available. Had a word or two just now with that nice couple on the top floor."

"Yes, sir." She smiled. "Lovely young people. But I don't know yet what Mr. Scale's arrangements will be. It's—Mr. Fuller had to go before his lease was up. Of course Mr. Scale would probably like to get a tenant in now, if he doesn't mean to be here himself. I don't know. You'd better write him. I'll give you the address, if you'll just step in." She added, as Gamadge passed her and she closed the door: "Mr. Scale always wants to settle about tenants himself."

"I understood that he does like personal recommendations."

"Yes, sir. I don't think"—she smiled at him—"that there'd be any trouble if you knew somebody he knows; as you would, I'm sure."

Gamadge said: "Very likely. Could I just see the apartment, Mrs. Flynn? Then I'd know better what I was bargaining about, wouldn't I?"

She hesitated. "It's neat enough, I cleared it up myself; and Mr. Fuller was a very clean tenant, and he wasn't here much. But Mr. Scale let it just as it was, and didn't do any decorating and repairs—Mr. Fuller wasn't particular."

"I don't think I'm over-particular," said Gamadge.

"Oh, it would have to be fixed up for a regular tenant, sir. It needs a good deal done to it. Mr. Scale was used to the old ways, he didn't care; and this Mr. Fuller—he only got the place as a favour, you might say. To oblige old Mrs. Woodworth."

Gamadge had such a shock this time that he actually had to put out a hand and clutch the polished old banister of the stairs. Fool! he thought. The landscape gardener. He said: "Mrs. Ames Woodworth; she died."

"Yes, poor old lady; she was an old friend of the Scales'. There's nothing Mr. Scale wouldn't do for Mrs. Woodworth, so when she wrote and asked him if this Mr. Fuller could have the apartment till October—"

"Year's lease, was it?"

"Yes, sir. Only Mr. Fuller was called away, way out West."

They were mounting the first flight of stairs, Mrs. Flynn in the lead. "He only wanted it for weekends now and then," she went on. "Or a day now and then in between. He got himself some kind of a houseman, only I never saw him. I'm only here at noon in the summer, and morning and evening in the winter months."

"Fuller, Fuller," said Gamadge, as if thinking aloud. "Man in his thirties, brown hair, glasses, tanned complexion, rather a sporty dresser. Could that be—"

"That's him," said Mrs. Flynn placidly, as they began the second flight. To her urban experience Mr. Fuller would be no cause for wonderment or disapproval. Anything in human shape could materialize on a New York doorstep with letters of recommendation; anything at all, nowadays. Types from the Village, from outlying centres of art, from foreign lands.

"Landscape gardener, wasn't he?"

"Yes, sir; and a lovely job he did in our yard. I mean he ordered it; I had it done myself through our own florists."

"Off on other jobs when he wasn't here, I suppose."

"Oh yes, sir, and then he got this wonderful opportunity in the West, and he went off."

They were on the second-floor landing, in front of a brown panelled door. "At a day's notice?" asked Gamadge casually.

"A week's notice, sir, he waited till the first of August; and he paid me up to October. A nice gentleman."

"If I came in, you'd refund his September rent to him, I suppose?"

"Well, sir, Mr. Scale would. I haven't the address."

She opened the door and allowed Gamadge to pass her into a big panelled room with built-in bookshelves and a fine old marble fireplace. "It was the old library," she said.

"Comfortable." Gamadge looked round him at threadbare upholstered chairs, old mahogany, old-fashioned lamps with battered silk shades, Rookwood urns on the mantel, an ormolu clock. The white ceiling was smoky, the rug faded and worn. "I'm not too particular for this," he said with sincere admiration.

Mrs. Flynn was pleased. "That's what I think; it would be a pity to change it. But it does need painting. And it's the plumbing and so on..." She led the way into a passage corresponding to the one in the flat above.

Her apology was called for. The kitchen was in bad shape—drainboard rotting, sink beyond polish, pipes rusty, woodwork of dark oak, with sinister cracks in it. There was an ancient drip icebox. Gamadge turned to look into the bathroom.

White enamel here, but rust from the pipes had discoloured it with reddish-brown stains; looking down into the tub, he had macabre thoughts:

"It can be done, I suppose; it has been done. But it never worked out well."

Mrs. Flynn spoke behind him: "Mr. Scale would have to put money into it. Unless a tenant wanted it at a low rent. I wouldn't advise that myself, the place needs doing over."

"Well, yes, it really does."

The bedroom was pleasant, and would have got plenty of sunshine if the sun were out. Grey clouds, however, covered the sky; Gamadge, leaning from a window, saw the garden closer now, its petunias soft-coloured in the softer light. Mrs. Flynn, beside him, said they were lovely flowers.

"Yes. Wouldn't think they'd grow so well in such sour old earth. I did something of the kind once, and they had to dig two feet down to put in enough new soil."

"They did here, sir; Mr. Fuller was very particular about that."

"He would be, of course."

"A terrible mess, sir; and then to think he had to leave!"

"Long job, too. You said he left on the first of August?"

"Last of July, sir. Yes, it was terrible—you know what workmen are. He ordered it done on—let's see—the Monday; July eighteenth. By Friday they had it ready, the whole border dug up. Then they quit for the weekend, and it wasn't till the next Monday that they filled in and planted the flowers."

"You mean you had the soil piled up around that trench, and nobody touched it on Saturday?"

"That's right, sir; and it took two more days to finish. One thing, they didn't hit rock, or clay either. It's a kind of sandy soil."

"They were luckier than I was. Fuller didn't returf, I see."

"They wanted to, of course, but Mr. Fuller said he'd leave it till spring. He'd spent a lot of money—I know how much, I paid the bill for him. He was great for cash, Mr. Fuller was."

"What a man."

He drew back into the room, glanced rather casually at the ponderous walnut furniture, said a little paint and plaster would do here, and that you'd never know there'd ever been a tenant in the place.

"Mr. Fuller didn't leave a collar button!"

"I suppose not."

It must be the dullness of the light, she thought, that was making him look so grey; he spoke as if he were tired, too—this closeness in the air was enough to take the life out of anybody. She was surprised when he asked her whether she had time to show him the garden.

"I have, sir; it's what I'm here for."

They went down to the first floor, and then along the hall to a door at the end of it which she unlocked. They were at the head of green-painted wooden stairs that led down into the yard.

"Convenient," said Gamadge.

"Mr. Scale put them in."

Standing on the old flags below, Gamadge looked around, over the fence, at the blind windows beyond that would be even blinder after business hours, when shops closed and the night club was concentrating on its own affairs. To right and left of him extensions jutted out, shades drawn down for the summer.

"Mighty private here," said Gamadge. He was walking along the path, past the petunia beds, stooping to admire the flowers. Mrs. Flynn, behind him, nipped off dead leaves.

Turning the first corner, Gamadge paused midway of the border and bent over it. He pushed a plant aside, then another. Mrs. Flynn joined him.

"Do they look dry? I'll give them a good sprinkling while the sun's in, for fear it shouldn't rain after all. It might not. I try to slip in of an evening," she went on, "but I've not much time."

Gamadge was moving along a little, pushing back other plants. He said: "The earth is sunk a little here, isn't it?"

"Is it? I didn't notice."

"In a kind of oblong. See?"

Mrs. Flynn stooped too, not a thing she was likely to do more often than necessary. "I do see. That's a funny thing—as if they'd filled it in looser here."

Gamadge straightened, lit a cigarette, and stood looking down. He said: "They left the whole border dug out over the weekend of the twenty-second, you say. And the new soil here?"

She was looking at him in perplexity. "Yes, but—"

Gamadge met her troubled eyes quietly. "You know what happened on Friday the twenty-second, don't you, Mrs. Flynn? Everybody does."

Her lips formed words.

"Was Fuller here that weekend?"

She nodded, her face chalky.

"You know they're looking everywhere. Ought we—"

She cried out: "It can't be!"

"Sh..." He glanced up at the Steadmans' windows, but there was no one looking out between the white curtains. Mrs. Flynn's eyes were fixed in the sunken earth of the flowerbed.

"It does look like a grave," he said very low.

"It does. I'll call Mr. Scale."

"Tell you what, Mrs. Flynn; in your place I wouldn't wait even to telephone Mr. Scale. He wouldn't want you to wait. These are his premises, and he's put you in charge of them. I'm sure you must know every policeman on the beat, and the radio men, and half the people at the Precinct."

"I do, yes." Her firm lips were a straight line as she met his eyes.

"They'll keep quiet until they find out whether this is anything; they'll take you seriously."

"They will."

"If I were you I'd go round there now, and say what you've noticed here, and give them the information about the gardening operations, and the dates."

"Mr. Fuller—"

"If they find nothing he'll know nothing; and don't forget that his only reference is dead. Mr. Scale may not know a thing about him, and he may have taken in that old lady."

"That's so."

"And be sure to put those top-floor tenants in the clear from the first, won't you?" He waited until he knew she had taken this in. She looked up at their windows and nodded.

"They were out of town all that time, and their families will say so. And don't forget to say that they didn't come here till June, and Mr. Scale himself knows all about them."

"Yes, sir. I'll see to it. God help them, I wouldn't—"

"Don't think the police won't be interested. They'd try anything."

Her eyes wandered, she was not yet convinced; but suddenly, as if she had had a blow over the heart, she staggered and stepped back. "Oh God, they were related!"

"You mean Mrs. Woodworth and Alice Dunbar; yes."

With a glance of horror downward, she turned away. "I'll go now."

"That's right."

She began to run. Gamadge watched her climb panting up the wooden stair. He followed, walked through the hall, and stopped in the vestibule to look along the street. Mrs. Flynn, at a fast walk, was almost at the corner. He went to the opposite corner and took a cab home.

CHAPTER NINE

Conscience

GAMADGE HAD A BATH, changed into the brown worsted suit, and ate a cold lunch. It was spattering rain now, and cool enough for him to bear the weight of his lightest rain-coat; he put it on, put on a soft hat, and took a cab down to the Scale corner.

The street was parked double, there was a small shiny van in front of the house, and Gamadge recognized a tall man in blue serge and a smart felt hat, standing with others on the steps, as his old friend Detective-Lieutenant Nordhall, Homicide. Turning back into the avenue, Gamadge hailed another cab and was driven to Fifth Avenue and Fifty-seventh Street. As he rode, he had visions of newspaper headlines dissolving, front pages being reset for afternoon editions, radio announcers interrupting programmes to bring listeners a flash: *The body, said to be that of Alice Dunbar...*

He got out at the corner and walked west. At Miss Bransome's building he looked up; her front windows were both wide open, she was getting the coolness before the rain slanted and came in.

He did not rattle the elevator gate this time, but toiled up the four flights of stairs. Her door was closed. He rang. She peered out at him, her smock off and a checked apron on, her hair tied up in a bandanna.

"Here I am again, Miss Brandsome; as I promised. I have news."

"Oh! What is it?"

She let him go past her, closed the door behind him, and stood gazing up into his face. He said: "Let's go somewhere and sit down."

She went in front of him down the hall and into a pleasant bed-sitting-room; it was very arty, with a spatter-dashed floor in several bright colours, chintzes to match, a studio couch in the corner next to the door. There was a wall-kitchen with its Venetian blind rolled up, its sink piled with washed and drying pots and pans.

"I'm interrupting your work," said Gamadge, "but my news can't wait." He pulled up a chair for her, but she sank down on the edge of the divan, so he took the chair himself.

"Now don't be upset," he said. "Everything's under control. They've found her."

"Found her..."

"She isn't alive."

"Where? Where?"

"When I left you I went and had a look over that house—the one you followed her to, you know. She wasn't there to see any young couple; she was there to meet a man who called himself Fuller. He'd somehow persuaded old Mrs. Woodworth to recommend him as a tenant—the owner's away. He was alone in the place that Friday she disappeared, and over that weekend. He'd had the yard dug up for replanting."

Miss Bransome was leaning back and back until she half lay against the couch pillows. Her face had a greenish look.

"I pretended to be looking for a vacant flat." Gamadge was sitting forward, his hands clasped between his knees. "I got the superintendent to show me the yard. There was a sunken place; I think I know what must have happened. He killed her in the apartment on Friday, and that night he went out and dug a foot deeper. Nobody'd see him or notice anything, or if they did, there'd been digging in that yard for a week. He carried her out there and put her in the place he'd dug, and covered her up with the old earth. Then on Monday they came and filled in the beds with the new soil. They planted a lot of flowers."

She had closed her eyes. He looked around him, got up, and took a little ruby glass decanter and a glass to match it from a wall cabinet. When he removed the pointed stopper he smelled sherry. He filled the little glass and brought it to her.

"You'd better have this."

She sat up, took the glass from him, and drank the sherry.

"That's right," said Gamadge. "Have some more."

She shook her head. He put the glass and the decanter down on a table at the foot of the couch; she was sitting up very straight now, looking past him at the wall.

After a long pause she said harshly: "If I'd told, they might have caught him." She turned her eyes on Gamadge. "I suppose he left?"

"He left on the thirty-first of July. He stayed on there, with a good view of that garden, for a week; we're dealing with a strong character, Miss Bransome. I think anybody might be excused for feeling a little chilled at the thought of Mr. Fuller; don't you?"

"Why did he do it?"

"I don't know; let's worry about more immediate matters first. They won't find me, I was just a man looking for an apartment; I managed it so that the superintendent saw that sunken area for herself. And we needn't mind about keeping our own counsel now—we can't tell them anything that they don't know—or"—he smiled—"won't know. They'll get in touch with the people up at the Woodworth place, and they'll run into Mr. Fuller there. They'll be told all about him."

She asked in a trembling voice, "What did you mean, then—'worry'?"

Gamadge leaned forward again and spoke earnestly: "The news will be out any minute now; and when it's out Fuller will have it too. Don't think he hasn't been watching and listening for it. He was as sure as mortal could be that she'd never be found—or not until the Scale house and its garden were blasted out for rebuilding; and that won't happen until Scale is dead, if ever. He won't miss this news, wherever he is. And what will he think of when he hears it?"

She kept her eyes on him, puzzled and wondering now.

"I'm afraid he'll think of you, Miss Bransome."

"Me!"

"How else should Alice Dunbar's body have been found? If not through you? *He* won't think I was a casual flat-hunter; he'll realize only too well that nobody would have noticed that sunken grave unless they'd been looking for it. Why should they look for it? Why *did* I look for it? Because you sent me there, and so far as we know you're the only living soul except Fuller that could send me. She was found through you."

She sat with her hands clenched together in her lap; rigid.

"You and I know," continued Gamadge, "that Alice Dunbar would have died before she told you who he was, or even that she was meeting this Fuller, or whatever his name really is; she deceived you and lied to you and kept her secret. But can Fuller be sure of that? I'll tell you one thing; now that she's been found, he can't afford to be sure of anything.

"And we," he added, smiling at her faintly, "can't afford to believe that she didn't—as you phrased it—give you away. I think she did; I think he knew all about you and the painting lessons. It wouldn't mortify Alice Dunbar to tell *him*. Miss Bransome, surely you don't think I'm telling you all this simply to frighten you? I'm telling you so that you'll realize you mustn't stay here alone."

She nodded, her lips pressed tight and her eyes staring.

"You're alone in the place after business hours, and you can't keep everybody out because you're afraid to click your switch and open the front door. I suppose it is locked at night?"

"The man does it when he goes."

"Our friend Fuller wouldn't risk it in the daytime. Hanged if I'd like to risk the chance of his getting in somehow, lock or no lock; and that hall door of yours would be so much paper to him. And we can't very well invoke police protection for you, can we?"

She shook her head violently.

"He mustn't know where you are, and he mustn't think you've run away on his account, either; if he did we'd never catch him at all."

"Where can I go?"

"Well, though I'd like to offer you asylum, it wouldn't do; we mustn't seem to be connected in any way, and I'm not saying so merely because I don't want to be knocked off myself—though I'd rather not be."

She gave him the glimmer of a smile.

"Now *I* know a nice young couple," said Gamadge, returning the smile. "They're in the suburbs, and I'm sure they'd take you in; until you care to make other plans, or can come back."

She said: "I got myself into this, and I'm not making any fuss about it; but would it be long?"

"The whole police department is working on it, and they have something to work on now. But I can't say how long they'll be. Oh, by the way, would you let me have your keys to the place?"

She looked at him sharply.

"I mean," said Gamadge, "if he did come, it would be a pity to miss him, wouldn't it?"

"*You're* going to catch him!"

"I can't catch him; the police have to catch him."

"But if you get them here—they'll know about me, won't they?" She added grimly: "Let them. I've been such a coward—I never knew I'd act this way."

"It was tough. I still think you can stay out of it; in fact I'm pretty sure you can, unless he tells on you—and he'd be a fool if he did."

She got up, found her handbag, and handed him the two keys. "That's the front door one."

"Thanks." Gamadge, on his feet, smiled down at her. "I'll telephone, while you pack your bag."

"Now?"

"The sooner the better; then he won't be so likely to think you've gone on his account."

Miss Bransome suddenly sprang into activity. She dashed for the wall-kitchen, attacked the spots and dishes and stacked them away. Gamadge, meanwhile, sat down at her telephone. He asked for an out-of-town number. By the time he had it, Miss Bransome was clearing out her icebox.

"Sally?" he asked, when the connection was made. "This is Henry Gamadge… Fine. How are you, and how's Tom?… As usual, I want something… That's nice of you. You have a little guest-room, haven't you?… Well, I have a paying guest for you. Very nice lady, an artist, name of…" He looked at Miss Bransome, who was putting things in a paper bag in the garbage can.

She mouthed: "Vesey. My mother's—"

"Miss Vesey," said Gamadge into the telephone. "Could you take her in for a few days, until she can make other arrangements? It's an emergency, Sally. Truth is, I got her into a kind of an impasse, you know how I am, and she'd like a quiet—Sally, that's fine of you. Will it be all right with Tom?…"

Miss Bransome mouthed at him again: "I'd do my room and give her a hand with the work."

"She says she'll pull her weight, Sally. Now if you'd just look at your timetable, if you have one; she could catch a train in an hour…"

Miss Bransome, galvanized by this last observation, slammed the icebox door and rushed into the hall, returning with a suitcase. She tore off her apron while Gamadge finished at the telephone; he turned to her cheerfully:

"They're people named Welsh; they have a nice little apartment in Hillville, and Sally's going to meet your train. And Miss Bransome—I got you into this jam; I'd like you to let me pay your board up there."

"I'll pay my way."

"If you like. It won't be much, they live very simply. Just starting out in life. Welsh commutes, you won't have him underfoot much."

"I can get along with people."

"That's the spirit."

Gamadge carried the garbage can out of the flat, and set it down beside Miss Bransome's front door. When he came back Miss Bransome was cramming clothes and toilet articles into her suitcase. He lighted a cigarette.

"This Fuller," he said, "I suppose there's no chance that he ever saw you?"

She stopped packing to look at him in amazement. "I never met anybody they knew."

"That's good. What's the sister like?"

Miss Bransome shut the suitcase and snapped the locks. "Jazz and men." She ran for the studio, closed windows, pulled shades.

"Really." He watched her as she scurried back, panting.

"And not nice men anymore, Alice told me. Very ordinary men." She added: "It was that wild Richfield Tanner."

"Introduced her to the wrong sort, did he?"

"Alice said the Air Force didn't improve him."

"She didn't like the men she met at the Stanton?"

"She wasn't asked to meet men there, you can be sure of that!" Miss Bransome was preparing herself for the journey by pulling on a sort of straw turban and a pair of yellowish gloves. Ignoring the mirror above her chest of drawers, she picked up a tan-coloured coat and said: "I'm ready."

"All set? Now if you'll just write a sign to put on your mailbox. Let's see: *Out of town, back tomorrow.*"

She glanced at him, went over to her desk, and wrote the message in large block letters on the back of a card. Gamadge took it from her, and picked up the suitcase.

She went over to the windows, closed them, locked them, said as if in surprise: "It's raining," and preceded him into the little hall. She opened a closet door, got out an umbrella, and joined him on the landing. She slammed the flat door after her as if finally and forever.

"Now you go down by the elevator, so-called," said Gamadge, "and I'll take the stairs. Nobody knows I've been here. You're just off on a country visit. I hate to have you lug this bag, but—"

"I'm used to it."

"Give me a minute before you shake the gate."

"You don't have to bother with me anymore. What's the train?"

"Three fifty-seven, lower level; but I'll see you into a cab."

Gamadge went down the stairs, waited between the first and second flight until he heard the elevator rattling past, and then went out into the vestibule. He fastened Miss Bransome's card into the slot beside her bell, and walked out and towards the corner. He stopped a cab, and waited with it until Miss Bransome hurried up to him.

"I've given our friend here a dollar," he said, and the driver grinned at him. "Here you go."

She paused with her foot on the step. "Will you call me?"

"I certainly will. From now on, all you have to do is sit tight and be surprised; just be surprised whatever happens, you don't know a thing."

"*They* might call me?"

"If we have any luck."

In the cab, waiting for the light to change, she let down the rain-splashed window to ask him with some interest: "Is there a reward?"

"Not for us."

"I don't feel so bad now."

"That's right."

The cab lurched away. Gamadge plodded to the corner with his hat over his eyes, crossed the avenue, and plodded on. He ended by plodding all the way home; he seemed to have found the only empty cab in New York for Miss Bransome, and the buses looked full. He was lying on the chesterfield in the library when the music on the radio stopped, and he heard the voice he had been waiting for:

"We interrupt the programme to bring you a flash from our newsroom. A body thought to be that of Alice Dunbar, missing since the twenty-second of July last, has been found by police buried in the backyard of a midtown apartment house. It has been provisionally identified by clothing, and by a hat and a handbag. Police are puzzled by the fact that the remains were wrapped in a red raincoat, which is said not to have belonged to the deceased. Further information will be heard over this station at our regular newscast on the hour."

CHAPTER TEN

Indescribable

AT HALF PAST six an apparition, still wearing its wet coat and hat, stood unannounced in the doorway of Gamadge's library and looked at him. He was mixing cocktails, and did not at first see his visitor, who gave the impression of being about to depart at any moment as mysteriously as he had arrived.

Gamadge looked up. "Hello, old man, glad to see you. Come in and have a drink," he said cordially. "Rotten weather."

Macloud took off the wet hat and cast it into a chair. Gamadge, shaker in hand, raised his eyebrows.

"Twenty-five years I've known this crackbrain," said Macloud, apparently to the ceiling, "and *still* he thinks I'm a fool."

"I don't think so at all."

Macloud addressed him loudly: "Do you imagine *I* think you're two people?"

"Oh. Well." Gamadge smiled. "No, I thought you'd remember our conversation on Sunday. I was—"

"Such a nice gentleman," said Macloud in falsetto, "but it's rather hard to describe him. We repudiate you," he continued violently, "so the police say oh well, the nice gentleman was probably a newspaper man looking for a feature story. At the

Scale house you were looking for a flat. Tell me one thing—where do you get all the suits?"

"Clara hoards them up in mothballs for me."

"You have the nerve to refer to our Sunday conversation; you said you weren't going to touch the case."

"I said I wasn't going to make a fool of myself," replied Gamadge, mildly. "And *you* said I could use your name."

Macloud made an angry sound. "You're withholding vital evidence in an atrocious murder case."

"My discoveries seem to have seeped through to the police, don't they?"

"You can stand there and quibble, but I've been to the morgue with poor Dunbar, and I had to stand by while Mrs. Dunbar checked the list of those rags her daughter was found in."

Gamadge walked over to him, dragged his topcoat off him, threw it over the back of a chair, steered him to the chesterfield, and pushed him down on it. He forced a cocktail into his hand, and then went out into the hall. Theodore was hovering at the foot of the stairs, appalled at the sound of Macloud's voice raised in anger.

"Come up and get Mr. Macloud's things," said Gamadge, "and dry them."

"He pushed right past me, Mist' Gamadge. What got into Mr. Macloud?"

"He's upset about the Dunbar case. Wouldn't you be?"

"Mercy on us. I forgot he was in it." Theodore came up and took away the hat and coat, casting a glance of pity and awe at Macloud as he left the room.

Gamadge poured himself a cocktail, and sat at the other end of the chesterfield. He said: "You know as well as I do, old boy, that a layman can't work officially, and wouldn't get anywhere if he did. And was I to let you in on my activities, which might not have turned out so well, and put you in the well-known uncomfortable position of pleading privilege? Or giving me away? I suppose you haven't given me away, have you?"

Macloud poured the rest of his cocktail down his throat. When Gamadge had taken the glass from him, and was refilling it, he said ominously: "Not yet. But I won't be a party to what you're doing now. I can see, damn it all, how you happened to go up to the Woodworth place; I admit you did talk about the two affairs as if there might be a connection. It sounded absurd to me, and I don't say I believe it yet. But how did you get to the Scale house?"

Gamadge said, handing him his filled glass, "There does seem to be a slight gap there."

"Yes. You'd better fill it."

"Suppose I gave you my solemn word of honour that that information wouldn't be of the slightest value, and that the source of it has nothing to do with the case?"

"Protecting somebody, are you?"

"The somebody talked to me in confidence." Gamadge leaned back in his corner and looked at the pale drink in his glass. "I have a couple of other reasons for keeping myself under cover for the time being. In a very short time I intend to go to the police myself."

"What reasons?" asked Macloud sourly.

"First, of course, personal safety. That always comes first, doesn't it?" asked Gamadge with a half-smile.

Macloud grunted. Then he said rather crossly: "If this Fuller can get his hands on you, we ought to be able to get our hands on him."

"Don't be ridiculous. We get our hands on people if we know who they are. My second reason for keeping out of it temporarily is the one I spoke of before—expediency. I can't move a step if I'm suspected by anybody of trying to collect evidence of any sort. None of these people ever heard of my meddlings with crime." He picked up an evening paper, and looked at the short paragraph of text under headlines half a foot high. "Mrs. Flynn acquitted herself nobly. I knew she would."

"She did. They got Scale long distance, and he gave them permission to dig the whole place up if they wanted to."

"Must have been a considerable shock to the old gentleman."

"He was gibbering. Very co-operative and sensible, you know, but furious that his place should be used like that, and that Mrs. Woodworth should have been used like that too. He never had any kind of communication with Fuller directly; Mrs. Woodworth wrote him that a very nice man she knew wanted a flat. She wrote in late September."

"Fuller didn't lose any time."

"No! Old Scale wrote to Mrs. Flynn and told her to let the fellow have it. Miss Cole finds him hard to describe, too; and Mrs. Flynn says she hardly ever saw him, and always in a poor light. Even when he first came, she was in that dark hall when she opened the door, and he had his back to the light."

"Neighbours?"

"Nothing so far, but it's early days. However, if he was going to commit a murder there, he'd take pretty good care not to be seen in that street."

"And Alice Dunbar took good care too?"

Macloud said morosely: "She might have been invisible, for all the police can find out about her comings and goings. And when did she come or go? Probably only that one time—that Friday. It's more of a mystery than ever. Those clothes."

"Yes, I was rather wondering about the red macintosh."

"She did some shopping that day; no doubt about it. There was a shopping bag buried with her; she'd stuffed it full of her own things—her gloves and stockings and handbag and hat—and she was wearing a lot of junk she must have bought and put on to disguise herself. Hat; cheap stockings and hat, God-forsaken pair of tin earrings, that red macintosh. The shopping bag had the name of a store on it, still decipherable; they'll probably trace the stuff to it. But that's still to be done. She was wearing her own dress and underclothes. They won't have to wait for her dentist to report—it's Alice Dunbar all right. The stuff in the shopping bag was in better preservation than the other things, of course. Twenty-five days in that grave: my God."

He drained his second cocktail. Gamadge reached for the glass, but he put it down and shook his head. "I'd be tight."

"You're staying to dinner? Theodore will manage something."

"Can't do it; too much on hand yet. I have to go back to the Dunbars'. You know what? Abigail Tanner ran out on us."

"What do you mean?"

"Well, she's back at the Stanton, you know, she's been there for over two weeks. She was up at the Dunbar house this afternoon, of course, after the news broke; but her mother has a nurse-companion—she's had one ever since Alice left—and there's nothing much for anybody to do, and Abigail said she was in the way. She left when I did, half an hour ago. I will say she looked pretty well knocked out."

Gamadge said nothing. He finished his drink, and asked: "Those people on the top floor—Steadmans—they're not being nagged too much?"

Macloud gave him a sideways, grudging smile. "First thing old Scale asked after the shock wore off. They're all right. Solid alibis, I helped with them myself. And they didn't mention any indescribable characters wandering around at the time of the discovery."

"I must be colourless to the point of transparence. But why mention me, after all? Nice people," said Gamadge reflectively.

"The architects and the printers and the stationers in that house are getting all the publicity they can stand, I tell you. There are a lot of people around town explaining now that they never laid eyes on Alice Dunbar. A mighty dangerous person to have known, until they find Fuller. That character certainly didn't leave anything behind him but Alice Dunbar's dead body and a few memories."

"Wonderful nerve he must have, to stay in the place until the thirty-first."

"Makes you think he *was* a maniac."

"Nothing else he's done points to insanity."

"That shopping she did—that disguise she put on—she certainly thought she was running away for good." Macloud shook his head gloomily. "I wish I could make sense of it. Why did he kill her? We had that all out before."

Gamadge said: "I won't pretend that I see a motive myself, not for Alice Dunbar's murder. But there may have been one for Mrs. Woodworth's, if we assume that the Dunbars did expect her money. I mean if they expected it to be left to Alice, the daughter who had no private fortune."

Macloud was sitting up, his face a study. "What's that you say?"

"Old Mrs. Woodworth won't be the first old party to fix a time bomb for her relations. Didn't you say she had her own lawyer? Would he think it necessary to inform the Dunbars that she'd changed her will?"

Macloud said blankly: "He'd never say a word. Close as a fish."

"The Dunbars won't think it a matter of life and death to save their faces about the Woodworth disappointment now. Go and ask them; ask Abigail Tanner, ask her intimate friends. I'll bet you anything that you'll find Alice Dunbar did expect a million when her great-aunt died, and that they had the shock of their lives when the will was opened."

Macloud was looking at him grimly. "I suppose this is something else you're releasing into the public domain?" He added, "It changes everything. It broadens the whole damned scope. That fellow with the long view—he may have thought he was getting the money for—any of them; if he killed Alice Dunbar after the Woodworth murder, I mean." Appalled, he shook his head as if to free it of the idea.

"We needn't feel that we must put a limit on his activities," said Gamadge. "We know what he's capable of, and we know he hasn't the normal complement of human feeling. I don't mean morals. I mean that he could live in the Scale apartment a week after he'd buried her under his windows."

"Yes, but—"

"Would it be too much of a strain on his conscience to shove an old lady downstairs?"

Macloud was thinking furiously. "Yes, but you're forgetting something. There's a catch. That will of Mrs. Woodworth's was published on the Thursday. Would he miss it? And it wasn't till the next Monday that he ordered that yard dug up."

"That's why I can't see his motive for the Dunbar murder," said Gamadge.

"There simply was none. Unless she told him about the will on the day she went to the Scale house—the twenty-second—and he killed her in a fit of temper." Macloud laughed shortly. "A whole week! It won't do. We're back at the old problem. How does her death benefit him or anybody?"

"At least we know that he may have thought it would benefit him to kill old Mrs. Woodworth. You must go up there, Macloud, and look at the terrain. *He* didn't go there just to get a reference for a flat." Gamadge put out his cigarette. "Is there any evidence how Alice Dunbar was killed?"

"There hasn't been time. It won't be easy."

"I know."

"If they can find anything like marks of strangulation, they'll be wizards. But that's a layman's opinion." He rose. "This rather looks as if Bruce Dunbar were out of it, don't you think?"

Gamadge pushed himself up off the chesterfield. "You don't see him killing a woman instead of jilting her?"

"That certainly; but the payoff is that Mrs. Flynn and Miss Cole would be able to identify him."

"They're so good at it."

"Fuller wouldn't risk it. He's nobody those two women could possibly identify."

Gamadge frowned. "Tan make-up, brown wig, glasses; I don't know. Clothes make a lot of difference too."

"Don't worry about Bruce Dunbar; we'll take care of him," said Macloud, as Theodore came to the door with his hat and coat. "You turn up Fuller for us."

"Is that an assignment?" Gamadge smiled.

"Go to it." Macloud was getting his arms into his coat sleeves. "Use my name."

"That's understood."

Theodore was smiling as he went down to the front door. He wished Macloud to realize that all was understood, all forgiven. Macloud asked: "Will you tell me the rest of it when we're ninety? Bridge that gap between the Woodworth place and the Scale house?"

Gamadge made a mental calculation. "When we're eighty, perhaps."

"I'll be waiting."

Macloud was out of the house, and the front door had slammed behind him, before Gamadge went back into the library and picked up the telephone.

CHAPTER ELEVEN

Call of Condolence

JENNINGS' "HELLO" WAS lugubrious, but there was a repressed excitement in it. "That you, Gamadge? Isn't this news horrible?"

"Awful, yes."

"I never had such a shock in my life. I bought a paper on my way home from the office, and when I saw that headline I stood there in the pouring rain and missed my subway express. And dear old Scale, everybody knows Scale; why, I've been to that house in the old days before he converted it. How he can ever live in it again…!"

"It's all very ghastly. Macloud was just here—"

Jennings' voice took on an avid note. "Had he any more details?"

"You'd have them from the family, I should think."

"Well, not yet. Of course I telephoned the house, I got that nurse-companion of poor Mrs. Dunbar's. She didn't know much. She told me that Gail was back at the Stanton. So I—but of course I couldn't ask questions. And it seems that the police are telling the Dunbars hardly anything. Doesn't that seem very brutal to you?"

"It's a murder case. I suppose—"

"Well, but is it?"

Gamadge was taken aback. "Isn't it?"

"Well, we don't know yet. Poor Abigail was wondering how Alice ever got into the place. Not like her at all. It isn't as if she had any—as if she could be meeting the man there. She didn't meet men. Not strangers, I mean; and he can't be anybody she *knew*."

"In that case it would be something of a mystery—"

"Abigail wondered whether she had got into the apartment by mistake somehow, looking for the printers—there's a shop there, and she had her gift cards printed, you know."

"I understood that they were all done by hand."

"Well, she might have had some of them printed; the family wouldn't know. And she might have run into some gang there—this Fuller was probably an underworld character, since he's completely disappeared. No forwarding address at all."

"Well, but then it is a murder case, isn't it?"

"Perhaps some accident. If she were frightened she'd jump out of a window."

"You tell Mrs. Tanner that won't do at all," said Gamadge. "Too much coincidence in it. Fuller may be a gangster, but he got his reference from Mrs. Ames Woodworth."

"It isn't too much of a coincidence, you know yourself such things are always happening. And if he recognized her somehow as Mrs. Woodworth's niece, why of course he'd threaten her—he'd be afraid she'd give him away. It's much more sensible, Gamadge, than thinking she had an appointment there."

"Why did she put on a disguise to go and talk to the printers?"

"Abigail says that's ridiculous, it wasn't a disguise at all. She went out shopping that afternoon, she was simply getting a few bargains. The things probably didn't look so bad before they'd been..." Jennings' voice died.

"Mrs. Tanner will have to do better than that," said Gamadge severely. "Mind you," he added, "I don't blame her.

It's a sickening thing for the family, but she'd better let it alone. How is she, by the way?"

"Well, I'm afraid she's in an hysterical state, Gamadge. It was all too much for her up at the house. She couldn't stand it. Miss Hooley, the nurse-companion, thought she was quite right to get off by herself, where she can be protected from the newspapers. Her father's busy, and her mother can't see anybody, not even Abigail. You know they brought things for her to identify? Mrs. Dunbar, I mean. She insisted—they wouldn't have made her do it, but she insisted. Gail couldn't stand it."

Gamadge made a sound that might have been one of sympathy.

"So she went back to the Stanton, where she needn't even get a telephone call if she doesn't want to. They do you very well at the Stanton, you know."

"She hasn't cut her telephone off yet, apparently."

"No, she's very lonely."

"I should think so."

"She's getting hold of Nellie Lynch, though. You know Nellie, of course? Very old friend of Abigail's. She's rushing right in from Jersey."

Gamadge had met Mrs. Lynch, a lively widow in her forties. He said so.

"It's particularly frightful for Abigail," said Jennings dolefully, "because she's so highly strung. There'll be the inquest, and they won't be able to have the funeral for goodness knows how long. I thought of calling up again and asking Nellie Lynch if I hadn't better go down for a little while later. I'm a very old friend, after all. Lawyer, too. It wouldn't look queer."

Gamadge was steeling himself; what he was about to do would mortgage his future. If Arthur Jennings ever got a foothold in a house he kept it forever; he was an old-fashioned caller and dropper-in, famous for getting past sentries, paralysing parties, out-staying everybody, exhausting his hosts. And Jennings had long shown unmistakable signs of wanting to get into the Gamadge house. His hints had been politely ignored, his invitations sidestepped; Clara, usually so charitable, couldn't bear him.

Gamadge said: "And it's such a rotten night, too; enough to depress anybody. Look here—how would it be if you persuaded her to slip out of the Stanton—they'd manage it for her—and come up here with you and Mrs. Lynch for a little while? Get right away from everything. I'm alone; we could have a drink, and if she wanted to hear what Macloud had to say, I could tell her. But I wouldn't mention it unless she did want me to."

Jennings was silent; the temptation—a double one—to spend the evening with Abigail Tanner for once, and to enlarge his calling list, was too much for him. He was trying to think how he could manage it.

At last he said: "I don't know, Gamadge. Of course it would be—you're an exceptional man. She'd like to meet you. But—well, I'll call her and see. It's very kind of you."

"Not at all."

Gamadge replaced the telephone. Theodore came in and began to lay the table for the evening meal. There was a long wait. Then the call came.

"Gamadge?"

"Yes."

"She was interested, and so was Nellie Lynch. We told her all about you." Jennings chuckled condescendingly. "Said you were quite distinguished. And she's very anxious to hear what Macloud had to say. But it seems that she has one or two other friends coming in to cheer her up, so she says we're to go down there, Nellie suggests about nine o'clock. They're having some supper in the suite."

"That's fine."

"You'll come?" Jennings sounded almost jubilant.

"Of course. If you can get as far as this in a cab, I'll drive you down. My car's outside."

"What a good idea. No cabs in this weather—I'll probably have to walk."

"I'll be ready by eight-thirty." Struck by a sudden and annoying idea, Gamadge called out: "Hold on a minute. You're not going to change, are you?" Never, he remembered, had he seen Jennings at the club of an evening in anything but his rather obsolete-looking dinner clothes.

Jennings replied stiffly: "I have changed."

"Artie, you're not human."

"It's purely habit. My mother expects it; so will Gail Tanner."

Gamadge rang off. He went and got into dinner clothes, had his supper, and listened to the radio until Jennings came. His rubbers were glistening with wet, his umbrella dripped on the mat.

"Short of service?" he asked in a housewifely tone of sympathy when Gamadge opened the front door.

"Theodore went out. Didn't you ever open a front door?" Gamadge was irritated already.

"To my knowledge, no."

Gamadge slammed the door, and they dashed for the car.

Traffic was heavy on Park Avenue; red and green lights were reflected mistily from the wet blackness of the pavement, yellow headlights came and went in the rain-dimmed oblong of the windshield. The wiper swept to and fro, Gamadge peered ahead, Jennings sat well forward with his hands on his knees and directed proceedings:

"Don't hurry, Gamadge; plenty of time."

"We're crawling."

"Look out, that cab is very close. I don't trust them."

"They're not looking for a crash."

"Don't hurry."

"I have to catch the light; if I don't, I'll hear from the army in the rear."

"It's really a very dangerous night for driving."

Gamadge said nothing. There was nothing to say, short of asking Jennings to get out and walk. After a pause he changed the conversation:

"What was Mrs. Tanner's husband like? As lively as they say?"

"I hardly knew him. One rather pathetic thing—Nellie Lynch says he was always so nice to Alice."

"Pathetic?"

"Well, if he'd lived he would have felt this so much. He always used to joke with Alice, brought her out."

"And took her out?"

"Well, no, I don't suppose so. He was wrapped up in Abigail. I mean he paid some attention to Alice—he noticed her."

Gamadge said: "This is all very dreary."

"The rain, you mean?"

Gamadge looked sideways at him, looked back, jerked the car out of the way of a car that had jerked out of the way of something else, and turned a corner. They drew up in front of the Stanton.

A uniformed attendant gave Gamadge a check, and drove the car into the parking place beside the hotel. The two went into a big quiet lounge, left their outer things at a counter, and crossed to the desk. Jennings, in a conspiratorial whisper, gave their names. Gamadge thought the clerk's glance at him was cynical.

They were announced, and walked to the elevators. The lounge was nicely got up for the summer in striped linens, with matching chintz in the long windows. "Attractive old place," said Gamadge.

"Oh, it's one of the best. The Dunbars chose it for her."

"I thought she had her own money and did her own choosing."

"Well, they'll leave her a lot more if she's good," said Jennings paternally.

The elevator let them out into a broad corridor, down which Jennings led the way. He stopped and rang. The door opened immediately, and they went into a large sitting-room that smelled like a bar and seemed full of smoke, music, and people. But there were only five people—the dark, bald man in a white mess-jacket and dark blue trousers who had opened the door for them, another man, handsome and fair, dressed like him, who sat at the other end of the room playing a piano, and three women.

There was a doll-like girl in pink, leaning on the piano, watching the musician, and an older woman in black whom Gamadge recognized as Mrs. Lynch, sitting on a loveseat to the right of the fireplace. Opposite her, on a similar loveseat, in a silk evening dress that billowed about her feet, was a haggard blonde who must be Abigail Tanner. She was leaning back with her eyes closed, her hair slightly disarranged against the cushions.

Mrs. Lynch sprang up. "Hello, Artie. Gail, wake up; here's Mr. Gamadge; you'll love him."

CHAPTER TWELVE

Informal

THE MUSIC WENT on; professional playing, with cunning hesitancies and recoveries, tuneless but rhythmical. Mrs. Tanner opened large blue eyes. They were bloodshot, the skin of her whole face was suffused and puffy, and yet the haggard look was there. She had not escaped through alcohol from the feelings that sent her to it.

She held out her hand. "Good old Artie. Mr. Gamadge. Wayne, get us something to drink."

The dark, bald man—he was only bald in front, Gamadge saw as he turned—was moving slowly towards a buffet that seemed to bristle with bottles, glasses, siphons; Mrs. Lynch said rather hurriedly: "Introductions first, darling, you know. Arthur, Mr. Gamadge, you must meet these nice people."

The dark man had an expressionless face, good-looking in a narrow-featured way. He might have been a good deal younger than he looked at first glance. He said in a flat voice: "Don't bother. Just part of the band."

"Now Wayne. Mr. Bishop is the leader of the orchestra, Mr. Gamadge. And that's John Osterbridge at the piano, and he sings too."

The pianist, playing on, looked up and bowed in a

mannered way, teeth flashing in a smile. His high forehead receded a little; he had a widow's peak. Definitely a charmer.

"And Dodie Bean, who sings too, and plays beautifully."

The little girl in pink was not very pretty, but she was made up to look so. She turned round eyes in Gamadge's direction, smiled vaguely, and then went back to her absorbed contemplation of Osterbridge's fingers.

Mrs. Tanner said: "Where're those drinks, Wayne?"

Mrs. Lynch glanced at Bishop, and then sat down and patted the loveseat. "Here by me, Mr. Gamadge. Artie, pull up a chair, and let's have a nice talk." Hardbitten, thin-faced, fashionable from head to feet, she looked good-natured, a good sort. Jennings, who had seemed a little at a loss, pulled up his chair obediently; but Mrs. Tanner waved the other suggestion away:

"If Mr. Gamadge is so wonderful, he'd better sit by *me*."

Gamadge complied, smiling at her. Bishop was looking at him, his changeless face showing nothing but detachment. He looked tired, perhaps ill. He asked: "Scotch? Rye? Bourbon?" and glanced at Jennings.

Jennings had crossed his legs. Sitting upright on the hard little white-and-gold hotel chair, he said formally: "Nothing for me, thank you."

"Oh, Artie," protested Mrs. Tanner. "Do you good."

"I'm afraid it doesn't."

"Can't burn it up?" Bishop did not insist. He looked at Gamadge again.

"I could burn up a Scotch and water, I think," said Gamadge amiably.

"That's right," said Mrs. Tanner, patting his sleeve. "Rye for me as usual, Wayne. Double."

Mrs. Lynch said casually: "I don't believe we need it, Gail ducky. I'm not having any. We're too nervous."

Mrs. Tanner raised her voice. "Double rye and let's see it coming."

Bishop mixed the drinks. The music went on. Jennings cleared his throat:

"The hotel orchestra isn't playing tonight?"

Bishop replied without turning: "Dinner's over. Dancing starts at ten."

"Music is so soothing, don't you think so, Mr. Gamadge?" Mrs. Lynch glanced towards Mrs. Tanner and back at Gamadge—a mighty good sort! As if at a cue, the music grew louder; there was a kind of tune in it now, sad and cynical.

Bishop came across the room with the glasses in his hand. Gamadge rose to take them, and Mrs. Tanner stretched out her hand. Bishop said, looking calmly down at her: "This one isn't going to do you a bit of good."

She was tilting it against her mouth before he had finished speaking. Half-turned away from her, he addressed Gamadge: "I'll collect my two, and in a minute or so we'll leave. Won't be missed."

Suddenly he smiled, and Gamadge was startled. Bishop had lost half his hair, he was ailing, he was as quiet as a cat and slow-moving, his unmodulated voice had as much expression as one piece of wood striking another; but he was a charmer too.

And with what a difference! No mannerisms for him. He didn't require them. In other words, Gamadge thought his smile was very attractive. He came from a tough background, he was probably tougher than these women could even understand, but let him turn that smile on them and he was the *homme fatal.*

Gamadge smiled in return. "It might be just as well if Jennings and I went too." He pivoted to see what Mrs. Lynch thought; she had been listening, and her face showed that she agreed with him.

"Might be better," she said, just above a whisper. "I ought to have known she couldn't go through with it. She was all right when Artie telephoned—she's only been hitting them up since then."

Jennings said nothing. His knees close together, his hands clasping the arms of his chair, he had a pitiable look of restrained horror. Bishop went back to the buffet, and picked up a tall glass which was half full of soda water just tinged with liquor. He lifted it to his mouth. Mrs. Lynch's eyes were on him.

"He can do anything," she said. "Play anything, sing. He oughtn't to be here at all—this is a small band. But he picked up some kind of a bug on his world tour in the war, and he can't stand a racket and late hours yet. Here they play only until one."

Mrs. Tanner called out sharply: "Mr. Gamadge."

He sat down beside her again. She put out her free hand, and he thought she wanted him to take it; he took it obligingly, but that wasn't her idea after all. Shaking her fingers loose from his, she made a vague gesture.

"Artie said you said I mustn't talk so much."

"Talk all you like to your friends, Mrs. Tanner. Don't go on record with things you couldn't back up—or don't believe." He added, taking the empty glass from her other hand and putting it down beside him on the floor: "Nobody'd blame you, but you don't want to sound as if you knew something and were fighting it."

"Knew something!" Her eyes were full of terror.

"When you only know what we all know," said Gamadge.

"I don't know anything. I can't understand it." She leaned forward and towards him, and he leaned forward too; they spoke with their heads together, almost in whispers:

"Where would she get a red raincoat?"

"Bought it that afternoon. So Macloud tells me."

"Because she was running away? Wouldn't run away in red raincoat. Wouldn't be found..." She stopped, looked sideways at him, her mouth drawn. "Know what I was going to say?"

"Yes. Never mind."

"I do mind. Why shouldn't I say it? She wouldn't be found dead in a red raincoat. And still they go on saying it was my sister, Alice."

"They'll know for certain tomorrow, but I don't think there's a doubt of it, Mrs. Tanner."

"Well, then, that makes it all different. I don't feel the same about it now. I'll tell you something—my sister and I were not—" She hesitated over the word, but brought it out at last, slowly and intact: "Congenial. We were not congenial." Suddenly she raised her voice: "Hate 'pocrisy."

Bishop was finishing his watered drink. He set it down. "Well," he said, "there's the book of the rules. Have to keep them—that's not hypocrisy. Just makes things easier all round if you keep the rules of the game."

Mrs. Tanner began to laugh. "You old gambler, you and your book of the rules." She got up, holding on to the back of the sofa, and put a knee on the padded seat. "Stop that noise, will you?"

Osterbridge raised his hands from the keys and poised them outspread in the air. Miss Bean turned to stare, her mouth open. The room seemed to be wrapped up in silence. Mrs. Tanner began to slip away from the loveseat, her hands first, her knee. She crumpled all at once as if boneless, had fallen to the floor and lay there quietly before anybody realized what was happening. Gamadge was nearest, and got her up in his arms while Bishop was still coming across the room.

The others were on their feet. Mrs. Lynch said: "It's all right, she's collapsed, I expected it," and walked past Gamadge without looking at him. "This way, Mr. Gamadge, this is the bedroom, just bring her in here and I'll put her to bed."

Jennings mouthed: "Doctor."

"No doctor," said Bishop. "She'll be all right."

Gamadge carried her through a doorway, getting a glimpse as he passed them of Miss Bean's gaping face, Osterbridge's expression of incredulous shock.

Mrs. Lynch shut the door behind him, put on a light, and ripped a taffeta spread off one of the twin beds. Gamadge stood waiting, glancing around him. It was an airless room, though the windows were wide open; a room with no personality, done up in orchid and green—hotel taste, hotel furniture. He laid the almost childlike weight on the bed, and he and Mrs. Lynch, side by side, looked down at her.

"Sleep it off, won't she?" asked Mrs. Lynch.

"I should think so; but you'll stand by?"

"I'll stand by. I stood by when she got the news about Rich Tanner. She didn't carry on like this." Mrs. Lynch lifted her eyes to Gamadge. "I wonder if she isn't suffering a little bit from 'ree-morse.'"

"Don't think so."

"Just general shock? Well, perhaps. It's enough to kill a buffalo, all this. I'd say Gail was pretty tough, but—you know something? In her place I wouldn't feel so much remorse about Alice."

"No?"

"No. She was morbid. You couldn't do a thing with her, not after that man walked out on her." Mrs. Lynch began to unfasten the straps of Mrs. Tanner's slippers. "I hope this doesn't get around; they don't need any more scandals now." She took the slippers off, went to the door, opened it, and called: "Beanie!"

Miss Bean appeared, looking reluctant and frightened.

"Give me a hand," said Mrs. Lynch. "I want to get her to bed. Thanks, Mr. Gamadge; good night."

"Anything I can get you?"

"Oh Lord, there's everything right here in the bathroom cabinet."

Miss Bean gazed without sympathy at the figure on the bed. "Is she tight?"

"She was exhausted," replied Mrs. Lynch with dignity. "Would you be surprised at that? Haven't you any feelings yourself? If this had happened to your sister, you might be laid out yourself."

"I'd be with my family, if I had one. Why isn't she with her family, instead of drinking in a hotel suite with a lot of men? I think it's awful, and Jack Osterbridge thinks so too."

"It doesn't much matter what he thinks or what you think either. And I'd keep quiet about this if I were you," said Mrs. Lynch with an intimidating glare. "The hotel wouldn't particularly like it if you talked around."

"I'm not going to talk around," said Miss Bean in a lower voice. "Jack says what she needs is black coffee."

"Black coffee!" Mrs. Lynch's black eyes snapped. "What do you mean, black coffee?"

"To bring her around. He says he can do it."

"He's insane. Bring her around? I hope she'll sleep till tomorrow afternoon. I hope she'll sleep a week."

Gamadge was at the door. "I'm going down to the dance room for a while, Mrs. Lynch. Listen to this band. If you can get off later, would you care to join me?"

"Thanks, that's a good idea. I'll probably be there." She kicked her black net skirts out of her way and bent to a chest of drawers; Gamadge went out. He found Osterbridge standing so close to the door that the pianist had to step out of the way. He had the same startled and frustrated expression that he had had when Mrs. Tanner collapsed, and he spoke quickly: "How's she feeling now?"

"She isn't. She's asleep."

Bishop stood with one elbow on the end of the buffet, a cigarette in his hand; the cigarette had a long ash on it. He looked imperturbable as ever, but as Gamadge shut the bedroom door behind him the cigarette ash fell unnoticed to the carpet. Jennings was planted like a mechanical traffic post in the middle of the room, his arms hanging. He said in a hollow voice: "I'm ready to go if you are, Gamadge."

"Oh, Artie, I'm sorry. I told Mrs. Lynch I'd stay and listen to Mr. Bishop's band for a while. They'll get you a cab, but if you'd rather, I'll drive you home and come back."

"That's all right," said Jennings, with cold resentment. "Just as you say."

He walked out of the suite, closing the door behind him carefully. Bishop followed this exit with his eyes, and then turned them back on Gamadge. He said gravely: "I don't imagine the guy ever saw a drunk lady before."

"Too bad about him." Gamadge was irritated.

"It's a kind of a mystery, isn't it? This killing." Bishop

raised his cigarette, looked at the quarter-inch he held, and dropped it into an ashtray. "And what does it get us? The fellow might be a thousand miles off by this time."

"He may not be."

Bishop was interested. "Why not?"

"He didn't think they'd find her. If he thought there was any chance of that, he wouldn't stay there for a week afterwards."

"I wouldn't in his place," said Bishop.

"And if they never found her, they wouldn't look for him; among Alice Dunbar's friends and acquaintances, I mean." Gamadge went to the buffet and poured himself a short drink. He swallowed half of it, and went on: "Miss Cole at the Woodworth place might recognize him, so might Mrs. Flynn. They have something to work on now; they might get somewhere."

Osterbridge had been looking at the bedroom door. Now he turned, and said loudly: "I told Beanie to tell Mrs. Lynch to try some black coffee."

"Yes," said Bishop, looking at him with a faint show of astonishment, "we heard you."

"I mean it's ridiculous; I never saw anybody crash like that all of a sudden—couldn't believe my eyes. It's more of a faint. She'll come around in no time."

Bishop questioned Gamadge silently.

"She's out for hours," said Gamadge.

"But she wanted me to come back in the intermission." Osterbridge's face had a stupid look. "We had it fixed for me to come back."

"Just a quiet talk, the two of you?" Bishop had a different kind of smile, and he used it now.

"Sure, like always."

Bishop, hands in the pockets of his well-cut trousers, sauntered over to the bedroom door. He rapped sharply. Mrs. Lynch's voice called after a moment: "Yes, what is it?"

"Send Beanie down in time, will you? It's more than a quarter to, and she's on ten minutes after we start."

"All right. Now go away, all of you."

Bishop came back across the room to stand with his fingers on the knob of the other door. He said: "Sounds like business. Come out of this, Jack, she'd have the house detective up as soon as look at you."

When they were all walking down to the elevators, Bishop addressed Gamadge politely: "You're really coming to catch a few numbers?"

"I'd like to. It's early." Gamadge smiled. "I didn't know the party was going to break up so soon."

"Spoiled your evening, too."

Osterbridge pushed the bell. Gamadge asked: "Nice place to work?"

"From my point of view it is. The place caters to a quiet crowd, mostly out-of-town people that come back year after year; middle-aged ladies or couples. But kids come in and dance, we have a good bunch every night."

The elevator came, and they all got in and rode down in silence. In the lobby, Bishop said, smiling: "You go along there and turn that corner; or do you know the place?"

"I don't at all, I've only lunched here in the main dining-room and the garden."

"No garden tonight." He turned in the opposite direction, and gestured towards a passage down which Osterbridge had already disappeared. "For the help," he explained, and walked away.

Gamadge stood looking after him for a minute, and then turned left, rounded the corner, and went along a broad corridor to the supper-and-dance room.

CHAPTER THIRTEEN

Request Number

IT WAS A well-proportioned, pretty room, done in pale red and silver, very modern. The french windows were screened against the rainy night with silvered reed blinds; Gamadge realized that the celebrated garden must be beyond them. It was a big garden, running back from the parking lot to the next street. A good place to sit between dances on a pleasant night.

The small stage at the far end of the room was already lighted, and the tables that ringed the dance floor were well-filled. They were comfortably spaced, too; the Stanton was not fashionable enough to pack the people in.

It was early, and there were still some empty places. Gamadge was seated (at his own request) to the left of the doorway, at the rear of the room. He ordered a drink, and surveyed the company. The middle-aged ladies and couples were there, very handsomely turned out, too; so were some of the young people, with or without their families.

The seven-piece band came on the platform, natty in their white coats and dark blue trousers; Osterbridge sat down at the piano. Then Bishop appeared, cast a serene glance over the audience, favoured it with the attractive smile and a half-salute with his baton, and leaned up against the left side of the proscenium. He pointed the baton languidly in the direction of the bass fiddle, the fiddler tapped and stroked out a rhythm, and the band was in full swing.

It sounded all right to Gamadge. He leaned back, watched the dancing, and sipped his highball. Bishop looked casual, but he had the whole thing in the hollow of his hand.

The dance ended, and Miss Bean came on the stage; she was quite pretty under the light they gave her. She sang, and Gamadge could only wonder how her smallish anatomy could produce the deep sounds of woe that proceeded from her larynx. The audience seemed to like her, and applauded until she gave an encore. Gamadge got the attention of a waiter, and handed him a card.

"I wonder if Miss Bean would like to join me after she's finished. Not against the rules, I suppose? I've met her socially."

The waiter looked considerably surprised; perhaps Miss Bean was not besieged by admirers in front. He took the card, however, and hurried away with it. She ended her song, smilingly bowed, left the stage, and the band lights came on again. In a few minutes she appeared in the doorway at Gamadge's right. He got up.

"Mighty nice of you, Miss Bean, to take pity on me. Here I am," he said, "trying to make an evening of it. I didn't get a chance to see much of you upstairs."

"No, it was a shame." She sat down and glanced about her. "We don't do this much here, it's just a quiet kind of family place, you know. Nothing conspicuous."

Gamadge resumed his seat. "Nice place, though."

"A stepping-stone," said Miss Bean, with her tight smile.

"Well, let's see. What would you like?" Gamadge passed her the supper menu. "There seems to be a speciality in the way of drinks, a summer punch they call it. Would you—"

"Just lemonade, please; artistes can't do much drinking, you know; not if they're serious."

It wasn't a whisky contralto, then, thought Gamadge. My God, what was it? He said: "You can eat, though, can't you? Or do you sing again too soon?"

"Not till after the intermission. I'd love a sandwich, one of these."

These were club sandwiches: Miss Bean was at least not going to stint her appetite. Gamadge ordered one, and the lemonade.

"I hope you have plenty of time for it," he said.

"Oh yes, the intermission comes at eleven. They give us half an hour, because people like to eat something then."

Gamadge felt as if he had cut a slice of eternity for himself and a young lady in pink. But she added: "I have to go behind pretty soon, though; I don't know yet what Jack's going to sing tonight. I accompany him, you know."

"I didn't."

"He's very talented."

"Yes?"

She waited a minute, and then said without looking at him, "That's why Mrs. Tanner likes to have him come up there—in the intermissions, you know, when she has people in; evenings when she doesn't go out herself. He can do imitations. He's very interesting."

"Is he? I should have said Mr. Bishop was the interesting one of the two."

She faced him quickly. "Oh no! Jack's been to college, he's been in the theatre—musicals. This is just a—"

"Stepping-stone." Gamadge, always rested by platitudes, had relaxed in his chair. The sandwich and the lemonade came, and Miss Bean fell to with zest.

"How long's he been here?"

She looked up, swallowed, drank some lemonade, and said: "Only about a year. Longer than I have."

"Bishop too?"

"Oh, he's been here ever since the war. He likes it."

Gamadge allowed her to enjoy her supper in peace for a while; quite obviously she was a single-hearted woman, who could not even pretend interest in any man but one. Must he begin to feel sorry for her? Hoping that he needn't, he asked: "What's the schedule here for the band? Lunch music, tea music, so on?"

"Not in summertime. I mean they do play at lunch, but not after that. In winter they play from four to six, but I don't sing. I can sing anywhere else I like."

"That's good," said Gamadge vaguely. After another pause, during which she finished the last corner of the sandwich and emptied the lemonade glass, he asked another question: "How did you leave Mrs. Tanner?"

She put down her napkin. "I shouldn't have talked like that up there. It wasn't nice of me. But it does make me so mad to see people behave like that." Miss Bean looked at him primly. "I think people get out of life what they put into it."

"Oh no," said Gamadge. "That one's no good."

"Pardon me?"

"They put a lot of fun into it, and sometimes all they get is grief."

"I mean spiritually."

"That's the stuff, you remember that if things seem disappointing later on."

Miss Bean, bored by her own sermon, had been looking about her again. Now she rose hurriedly, said thank you ever so much, she'd had a lovely time, and made for the doorway. She went through it sidelong, passing Mrs. Lynch without visible signs of recognition. Mrs. Lynch came in, saw him, and approached laughing.

"She thinks I'm the devil. You been entertaining her? Fast worker." She slipped into the chair next his. "Hope you liked it."

Gamadge sat down. "I rather like to talk to different kinds of people. Where's a waiter? Oh, there you are. What are you having, Mrs. Lynch?"

"Nothing for me."

"Great Heavens, Jennings ought to be here. He'd get all his illusions back again. Miss Bean drinks lemonade. Won't you have some root beer even?"

"Oh well, a Tom Collins then. Thanks. Did Beanie sing a request number?"

"I don't think so, I didn't hear anybody *ask* for the thing."

"It's a homey way they have at the Stanton. After the first song you can request something; John Osterbridge knows everything. It's quite a regular clientele, you know; most of these people have been coming here for ages, and they're very fond of the band."

"When does Osterbridge give out?" asked Gamadge gloomily.

"Just before the intermission." Mrs. Lynch was perched in a fugitive kind of way on the edge of her chair. When the waiter had removed Miss Bean's plate and glass she clasped very white and ringless hands on the edge of the table, looked down at them, and said: "I can only stay a few minutes. Gail's all right, sleeping the sleep of the just, but I've got to get back."

"You'll certainly be needed tomorrow when she wakes up."

"I'll be there with first aid. But what I mean is, I got hold of a nice maid that takes care of the suite, and she's sitting for me, but she needs her sleep and I can't ask her to stay late. And I got the house detective to hang around up there, see that nobody rings the bell." She glanced at Gamadge. "That Osterbridge!"

"He undoubtedly wants a word with Mrs. Tanner."

"Thinks he's so soothing. I really came down because I wanted to ask you not to think anything of it; I mean these people"—she raised her eyes to the bright platform across the room—"they're just entertainers to Gail. I mean she likes them personally, too, but there's no intimacy. Not that there'd be any harm in it; she rather enjoys different kinds of people—as you do." She smiled at him.

"They must be quite a change for her."

"Do you happen to know the family? No? Well, if you did you might understand that she'd like anybody who was as different as possible. I know she ought to be at home, but they're the kind of people that have to have prestige, or they're helpless. They go on and on, asking why, asking what they've done to deserve it. They can't face things. I'm just explaining."

"They'd be trying. Somebody else was saying so recently."

"Anybody'll tell you." She was looking at Osterbridge, who swayed to and from his piano like a reed in the wind. "Poor John is rather a phoney, I suppose."

"But Bishop's the real thing."

"Yes, he is." She frowned at Gamadge. "I know what you mean. But you'd be surprised how civilized he is in his own way."

"Would you care to cross him up?"

"I don't think he's so alarming. Oh Lord, that's thunder. Let's hope it clears the air. I hate this weather."

A voice behind them said: "Hello, Nellie; may I sit down?"

She twisted to look up. "Bruce darling, where did you spring from?"

"Well, are you surprised that I caught a train?"

Gamadge had risen. Mrs. Lynch said: "Mr. Gamadge, Mr. Dunbar. He's a friend of Artie Jennings, Bruce. Artie brought him down, but poor Gail gave out and people had to leave."

"They said at the desk that she was in bed, and that you were staying. And they sent me in here."

"Yes, I told them where I'd be."

Dunbar had hardly looked at Gamadge yet. Now he turned to him and they nodded. A well-set up young man, thought Gamadge, good-looking, full of vitality. He said: "Do have a chair, Mr. Dunbar, and something to drink."

"Nice of you." They sat down, Dunbar on Mrs. Lynch's other side. He asked: "Gail all right? I mean of course she can't be, but is it serious?"

"I'm afraid she just passed out, Brucey."

"Very wise of her." He became aware of a waiter hovering, and said: "Double Scotch, please, with water."

Gamadge caught his eye. "You'll rather wonder where I fit in, Mr. Dunbar. Only as a friend of Bob Macloud's."

"Oh yes. You know him?"

"Very well. He was up at my place this afternoon, and Mrs. Tanner wanted to hear what he had to say. I really couldn't tell her more than she knew, but people always think the police are keeping things up their sleeve."

"Why should they? They told me all they knew, over long distance, as soon as they found her—found my cousin Alice." His agreeable face was sombre. "It'll kill them, Nellie; the old people. I went straight up there." He smiled without amusement. "Had an escort. They met me at the train."

"Why on earth?"

"They have to do things like that. But they'd picked me over pretty thoroughly before, so there wasn't much more they could ask me—only about a million questions over again. The trouble is there's no answer to the big question—why?"

"Oh, Bruce, it's a nightmare."

"Isn't it, though? Well, they told me Gail was back here, so down I came. Poor old girl, she has more feelings than people give her credit for." He glanced up at the dancers, and his eyes moved to the stage where the band played with energy. "Those the bums she likes so much?"

"They're not bums, Bruce," protested Mrs. Lynch. "At least Bishop isn't, or the man at the piano. Those are the only ones she knows at all."

He gave her a faintly amused look. "I didn't suppose she was teaming up with the drummer. Funny thing," he went on, studying the band again, "they never can learn how to dress."

"They're very smart, Bruce, you know they are!"

"The beautiful character at the piano looks as though he wore corsets."

"Richie was the one that knew all the jazz artistes and took Gail around."

"That so?"

The waiter came with his drink. He lifted it in Gamadge's direction and smiled. "Next on me." He drank, set the glass down, and said: "That makes me feel better. Reason I chased in here after you, Nellie—they had some news up at the house, and I thought you'd pass it along to Gail tomorrow, if you'll be so kind. Then she won't get it from cops, and it may come easier."

"News, Brucey?"

"Yes." He glanced across her at Gamadge. "No secret about it, it'll be in the papers tomorrow morning."

"I'll keep it to myself until then," said Gamadge.

"If you will. You look as if you would, and how you come to be a pal of Artie Jennings, I don't know."

Gamadge said, raising his eyebrows, "Classmates."

"Oh. That accounts for it. I had some pretty damn funny ones in Switzerland." He glanced about him, then said in a low voice: "They've just found out how she was killed."

Mrs. Lynch's hands tightened on the table edge.

"She was shot twice in the back," said Dunbar in an expressionless tone. "Close range. They found the bullets in that apartment at Scale's—the Fuller place; in the wainscoting of the kitchen passageway. Old cracked wood, nothing showed until they really began to look. There's no window there, so that's why the shots weren't heard. It's a well-built old dump, they weren't noticed above or below either."

"Oh Bruce." Mrs. Lynch was very pale. "Will that help them?"

"Well, the bullets came out of a thirty-eight-calibre automatic. They're that much further on."

The dance music stopped, Osterbridge got up from the piano and came to the front of the stage, Miss Bean fluttered on from the wings; she smilingly took Osterbridge's vacated place in front of the concert grand.

"Oh God," muttered Dunbar, "is he going to sing?"

"Looks as if he was going to sing a hymn or something," said Mrs. Lynch. "What's the matter with him?"

"You know," said Gamadge. "He wanted a private word with Mrs. Tanner and he isn't going to get it—until tomorrow."

Dunbar's expression showed nothing beyond a faint surprise.

"Don't be so uppish," said Mrs. Lynch irritably. "If *she* isn't, it's because she has a good heart. Perhaps you don't know that I was about down to my last cent once, and no fault of mine either. It was Gail Tanner that came through with the cash—cash, mind you. Do you see much of that laying around at the disposal of hard-up friends nowadays? And if you think she wasn't kind to Alice, Bruce—"

"She was rotten to Alice."

"All right, that happens in families."

"Shush, we might miss some of the bel canto."

They sat while Osterbridge crooned mournfully. He had great applause, and then stood as if waiting, a sad smile on his face; Mrs. Lynch whispered: "Request number. Any requests, boys?"

"Request?" Gamadge leaned forward and bellowed cheerfully: "Stephen Foster! Stephen Foster!"

Mrs. Lynch jumped in her chair, Dunbar looked at him in pleased astonishment, people turned their heads and smiled. But the band seemed at a loss. Osterbridge stood looking in the direction of the petitioner, his mouth slightly open. Bishop, in profile to the audience, leaned back with a hand in his pocket, his baton idly swinging. Miss Bean's hands were poised helplessly over the keys. The horn tried a ragged sequence from "Oh Susannah," and ceased.

Mrs. Lynch giggled: "You've got them stumped. They never heard of him."

"Only the nice man with the horn," said Gamadge. "Would you believe it?"

"No, and I can't stand it," said Dunbar, getting up. "Such inanity."

He began to sing in a clear, light, untrained baritone; as if he were doing something unimportant, inevitable, natural. Faces turned to him, everybody was smiling. A hand on the back of his chair, the other in his pocket, he went through the first stanza and refrain; the red rose dropped sweetness all over the room.

By the time he had asked the plaintive question: "Why should the beautiful die?" there had been slow tentative whines from the electric guitar, a note or two from the saxophone; the bass fiddle was gently beating out the rhythm. Bishop's baton was really swinging now; Osterbridge had taken Miss Bean's place at the piano and was trying chords. Now, at the end of the verse, Dunbar was about to sit down; but there was tumultuous applause, in which the band joined. Sentiment, recognition, fidelity to a national demi-god, had captured the audience.

Dunbar got up again, grinning from ear to ear. Bishop pointed his wand; Osterbridge played a chord; at first there was only a skeleton accompaniment from the platform, but at the last words: "Why should the innocent fear?" there was a crescendo and a roll of drums that would have startled Stephen Foster out of his wits. That ballad had never had such a finale. The audience was clapping wildly.

Dunbar exchanged mock-formal salutes with Bishop and the orchestra, Bishop tapped his baton against a music stand, and the band plunged into a lively dance tune. Dunbar, still standing, drank off the rest of his whisky.

"That was terrible of me," he said, "but I couldn't help it. I'd better go before anybody happens to find out who I am."

"Brucey," said Mrs. Lynch, who had tears in her eyes, "it was wonderful."

"Oh Lord, I've heard my mother sing it a thousand times. But I oughtn't—"

Gamadge smiled up at him: "Why should the innocent fear? I'm deeply obliged to you, Mr, Dunbar. And I really can't understand why Osterbridge, for instance, didn't know one song."

"They might know the songs, but not the composer," said Dunbar. "Just like them."

"Bishop, too. I can't understand it. Well, you saved me from making a complete ass of myself, anyhow." Gamadge stood up. "Must you go?"

"Don't dare stay; and I ought to get back to the house. I'm staying with the Dunbars." His face clouded again. "I have a key, but it wouldn't do to disturb anybody. We're quite a family." He smiled at Gamadge. "Gail passed out upstairs, and me down here entertaining customers. Nice for the Press."

He shook hands with Gamadge, patted Mrs. Lynch on the shoulder, and was gone.

Mrs. Lynch rose. "I'm overdue upstairs. Goodness, it's nearly eleven o'clock; they'll be having the intermission. I don't want the house detective pinching poor Jack Osterbridge."

Gamadge asked: "Did he know Alice Dunbar?"

She was startled. "Not that I know of. He might have. Why?"

"Mrs. Tanner said Alice didn't know any of her friends."

"Oh—did she?"

"Yes, it was in the papers after she disappeared."

"I don't know a thing about it," said Mrs. Lynch, and hurried away.

CHAPTER FOURTEEN

End of Evening

GAMADGE STOOD LOOKING after the departing figure of Mrs. Tanner's friend. "Repeat that if you like," he thought. "It certainly won't come as a surprise."

He was beginning to feel that he had had a long day; the music, good of its kind, was no more than a din in his ears; the motions of the dance, when he turned back to the room, looked to him like the aimless gyrations of dolls on wires. But his thoughts were still churning, if sluggishly, and he was as hungry as Miss Bean. Should he go home and investigate the icebox? He might find it uninteresting; Theodore's housekeeping, when Gamadge made these short trips home in the summer, was careful.

The intermission was coming; why not sit quietly down and eat something in peace while he regularized his ideas? He subsided again into his small but comfortable chair, consulted the menu, and ordered an egg-and-watercress sandwich, a ham sandwich, and coffee.

The band stopped playing and the musicians filed out. Bishop cast a look of inquiry towards the corner which had supplied the request number, and followed them from the platform. Some of the audience settled down to supper, many of them came past Gamadge into the lobby. His coffee and sandwiches were put in front of him.

Eating and drinking, he went over the events of the evening and back from them to the disappearance of Alice Dunbar; back from that, to Alice Dunbar's life with her family.

From the first, he had realized that her principal opportunity to meet men outside her own small circle would have been at the Stanton, among her sister's friends. She might easily have met Bishop or Osterbridge in Mrs. Tanner's suite, and followed up the acquaintanceship afterwards; the hours of her visits to the Scale house would be free time for these men.

After her disappearance, Mrs. Tanner had denied that her sister knew them; but after her disappearance Mrs. Tanner realized only too clearly what happened to men who had known Alice Dunbar. She had seen it happen to Bruce Dunbar. Because he lived alone, had a car and a private garage, didn't keep house, had no regular occupation to tie him down to regular hours, his life had been made a burden to him. It would be more of a burden now that the body had been found, and they'd be trying to connect him with the Scale house and Mrs. Woodworth; they wouldn't connect him with either, but they'd keep at it for a long time.

All this would be annoying and socially awkward, to put it very mildly, for a Bruce Dunbar; what would it have meant to a Bishop or an Osterbridge? Would their records, for instance, stand up well to it? Even if they did, would the management of the Stanton react favourably to it? Would the family custom? Now, of course—but even then, it would have been tough for the piano artiste and the band leader. Mrs. Tanner's large heart might have melted for them. Neither, of course, she would tell herself, could possibly have been interested in poor Alice, even if they had thought she expected money from her great-aunt Woodworth; she'd keep both or either out of it.

But now! She might still intend to keep them out of it, but she was certainly in a very hysterical, queer state, and she was drinking. She had made foolish suggestions about the murder to Jennings, the suggestions of a frightened woman who wouldn't face what had really happened. She had seemed frightened tonight—to Gamadge's thinking she had not shown remorse, but anxiety.

And there had been no sign of affection between her and Osterbridge; nothing even resembling love. Her tone when she ordered him to stop playing was enough to convince any moderately intelligent person of that, and Osterbridge himself had shown nothing of the sort either. He was frightened too.

If Gamadge was right, and he had met Alice Dunbar, and Mrs. Tanner knew that he had, he would certainly be wanting that private word with Mrs. Tanner tonight. She had been inaccessible before—with her family from the time of the discovery until the Stanton dinner hour, when the band would be playing. Osterbridge had counted on a few words afterwards; Bishop and Miss Bean wouldn't get in his way. But Mrs. Lynch was there, Jennings came and Gamadge came. The intermission, then.

And Mrs. Tanner had collapsed, and she would be inaccessible again until the next morning, when the police would probably be nagging at her once more. No wonder he had suggested black coffee.

If Gamadge was right, and that had been his trouble, he couldn't be checked up on any more than Dunbar could. The Scale house wasn't more than half a mile from the Stanton.

Gamadge finished his coffee, put his cup down, lighted a cigarette, and indulged himself in one last and fascinating conjecture: "The family wouldn't like it if Alice Dunbar complained of *him*. She'd complain to some purpose if he decided to transfer his attentions to her sister. After the Woodworth fiasco, Mrs. Tanner would be the better match, but she wouldn't get the Dunbar money if she married a singer who'd tried for the Woodworth money first."

Osterbridge looked like a man who thought himself invincible with the women. Would he believe that Mrs. Tanner could resist him if he decided to turn on the charm? A little later, naturally, not while the family was in the middle of a celebrated case like this one.

Gamadge sat smoking, looking across the half-empty room at the open concert piano on the stage; at the bass viol, the horn and cornet lying on chairs, the drums, the curving saxophone, the steel guitar. He thought of brown wigs over bald heads or light hair, of horn-rimmed glasses, layers of brown powder, plumpers and adhesive tape. He thought of dim rooms in town or country, of identifications and what they were worth.

And he thought of other things, things everybody knew or could know, and sadly shook his head.

As for the Stephen Foster business, what did it prove, what could it prove to anybody but him? That detail didn't seem to have been passed along by Miss Cole to others; she might have forgotten it, and so might the singer have forgotten it. If the singer remembered it, would Gamadge's naïve demand frighten him? If it did, he might react either way: boldly like Dunbar—"why should the innocent fear"—or with a pretence of ignorance, if that had been pretence on Bishop's or Osterbridge's part.

Nobody would be convinced either way. Bishop could say he'd forgotten the ballads and wouldn't give out with "Swanee River"; Osterbridge could say he'd forgotten the words. "No good to a soul on earth," thought Gamadge, "except me. And I'm prejudiced."

A voice at his shoulder whispered: "Mr. Gamadge."

He turned and rose. "Miss Bean?"

"Mr. Gamadge, Wayne Bishop sent me." She looked flurried. "He wants to know if you'd mind coming behind and speaking to him before the end of the intermission."

People were coming back into the room. A waiter slipped behind one of the silver screens and pushed open the leaves of the french windows; it must have stopped raining.

"Be there as soon as I've paid my check, Miss Bean."

"Oh, thank you. Wayne says you know the turning in the lobby, and then there's another passage on your right."

"I'll find it."

She gave him a look that had doubt and anxiety in it, and fluttered off. Gamadge looked at the check on the table, put money down on it, and strolled into the lobby. Past the elevators, he turned the corner into the plain druggeted corridor that seemed to lead all the way through the hotel to the rear. Halfway down it was the cross passage, which must run back of the stage.

There were three doors in the wall opposite the partition behind the stage, and another door at the end of the passage. Against this Bishop leaned, hands in the pockets of a raincoat that was hanging open over his uniform. The khaki colour of the raincoat and the bleakness of the light here may have been what gave him his sallow, almost pallid look. He said without moving: "This is very kind of you, Mr. Gamadge."

Gamadge walked towards him and stopped a yard away. He said: "I hope you didn't get me here to scold me, Mr. Bishop?"

"Scold you?"

"For requesting the wrong thing."

"Oh." They exchanged a smile. "That happens," said Bishop. "Makes us look silly, doesn't it? Osterbridge doesn't sing that kind of thing, and just for the moment I couldn't remember anything you'd want. I didn't suppose you'd want 'Susannah.' Who was the fellow that obliged?"

"Some friend of Mrs. Lynch's."

"Nice voice. Osterbridge said it reminded him of glee club days on the dear old campus."

"You all ended up nobly."

"Simple harmony; I liked it myself. Why did you ask for Foster, Mr. Gamadge?"

"Why do you ask me?"

Bishop's dark eyes left Gamadge's face and contemplated vacancy. "You had some reason—or I thought so."

"Don't you ever have an impulse?"

Bishop pulled himself upright. His voice changed and sounded businesslike. "I wanted a big favour of you. We go on in five minutes, and I can't find Osterbridge."

"Can't find him?"

"I'm just back myself. Went out for a drink—that way." He half-turned and indicated the door behind him. "It goes to the garden, short cut to the next street. There's a gate, you can't open it from the outside. It had stopped raining, so Osterbridge was out there, just beyond the door, having a smoke; I went on out to my usual tavern around the corner, and when I came back I couldn't seem to find him." He added: "I leave the gate ajar."

"He'll be back in time, won't he?"

"He was supposed to be back long ago, to talk to Beanie about his songs." Bishop turned and glanced at the middle door of the three in the wall. "That's our sort of greenroom. The men's dressing-room is next to the garden door there, and the women's is the one at the end. Beanie was in the middle room, talking to the band; he hasn't been there or in the dressing-room at all, not since the intermission started." Bishop looked at Gamadge again: "I thought he might have gone upstairs."

"Oh. I see."

"He was worried about Mrs. Tanner. He's a kind of character that if he wants a thing he makes every effort to get it, and he certainly seemed to want to talk to her. I don't want to go up there again, and I don't want to send Beanie. Mrs. Lynch might complain of us, and we get nowhere antagonizing the management of the hotel."

"Wouldn't Mrs. Lynch get rid of him?"

"He's quite persuasive. He never did anything like this before, but it's a sort of an upset evening. Beanie could play the piano for him, but she can't sing for him. He has quite a following."

"I saw that he had."

"Would it be too much to ask you to go up there and see where the bonehead is? I mean if he's in that suite?"

"No, not at all."

"It's a good deal to ask, but you could do it and no questions asked."

The band was coming out of the middle doorway. One by one they crossed the passage and mounted a short flight of steps to a masked door at the back of the stage. All of them had an inquiring look at Gamadge, and the horn player whistled a bar of "Oh Susannah" under his breath and grinned. Gamadge grinned back at him.

"Thanks," said Bishop. "I have to go."

He peeled off his raincoat, threw it into the middle room without looking to see where it fell, and followed the last of the orchestra up the steps.

Gamadge stood looking after him. The music started up, and Miss Bean could be heard pounding the piano in a serious manner. She must have gone up into the wings before Gamadge arrived in the passageway.

Did Bishop really think that Osterbridge would have been allowed into the Tanner suite again that evening? Gamadge thought that Bishop was incapable of thinking anything of the kind. He thought that he himself had received a pressing invitation to go out and investigate the garden.

"And he knew I'd go." Gamadge went up to the end door and pulled it; it was a heavy steel door, fitting into its frame like a glove. He stepped out into the dark of the garden; a rain-soaked and desolate confusion of piled-up tables and chairs, thick shrubbery, trees. On his right, behind the high palings of a fence, was the parking lot; the narrow walk on which Gamadge stood, a raised causeway, extended through a gate in the paling right through to the street, behind rows of parked cars whose metal bumpers glinted in the shadows beyond the range of the spotlight.

Activity there; figures on the walk, people waiting for their cars, getting out their checks. But on the left, along towards the hedge and fence that cut the garden off from the next block, nothing. The fence was high, a palisade of bars topped with spearheads; the hedge was thick. No light but what came vaguely from the street and from the distant parking lot.

Gamadge walked down towards the gate that Bishop had so carefully described to him; yes, it opened easily from within, but you couldn't get your hand through from the other side to turn the knob. Gamadge swung around and began to slowly walk back the way he had come, his eyes on the darkness at his right. Wet grass, wet flagstones, slim tree trunks, bushes, tables, and chairs. At the side door through which he had come into the garden he turned and walked back again to the gate.

This time, just within the gate, he struck a match and lighted a cigarette, his head lowered and his eyes on the shrubbery near the fence. Now he got it; just a suggestion of whiteness under that bush, beside that tree.

He threw away the cigarette and picked it up again; put it and the burned match in his pocket, and moved over the wet flags and the grass. Osterbridge lay under the bush, not far from the gate; or Gamadge supposed it was Osterbridge; he seemed to have shot himself through the right jaw, upwards. He had fallen after the rain stopped—his coat, sodden where it touched grass, was dry above.

The automatic lay near his right hand; it had bounced on the turf, and was glistening wet. His left arm was under him. The body had fallen forward, and lay in the peculiarly flat, final attitude that meant death; but Gamadge bent and touched the hand. Long-fingered, broad, powerful; dead.

Gamadge straightened, and cast a look of irony at the garden door. Quite an errand, he thought, Bishop sent me on. Damned if I'll oblige him.

He turned and went back through the door and into the deserted passage, along the passage to the corridor, back to the lobby. Plenty of people moving about there; he joined a small crowd at the counter and got his hat and raincoat. Out in the street he waited for some time before they brought him his car; waited on the raised walk, from which nothing could be seen of the garden, through the narrow gap in the paling, but darkness.

The fence jutted out too far for him to have been seen on that promenade of his to and from the gate; and when he crossed the flags, in his black clothes, he would hardly have been even a shadow to a man looking up at that moment, a man actually looking for him.

He got his car, drove west to the next avenue, turned the block, and drove east. On Lexington Avenue he found an open drugstore. He parked around the corner and went in. He shut the door of the telephone booth tightly behind him, and called the Stanton.

The switchboard girl said: "Hotel Stanton, good evening."

It was good morning, but Gamadge didn't correct her. He said as fussily as he could: "I should like to speak to the manager."

"Who is speaking, please?"

"That does not matter in the least. The matter is urgent, and I wish to speak to the manager."

He was switched on to a man, probably the night clerk. The night clerk asked: "Who is speaking, please?"

"I am—I was a temporary guest of the hotel. The matter is urgent, and the manager will be glad to keep it private."

He could almost hear the clerk's patient sigh. "I will give your message to the manager of the hotel."

"It's your responsibility. I am merely performing my duty as a citizen," said Gamadge. "I ought to be on the manager's private wire. It would have been simpler for me to inform the police, but I was anxious to get home to bed."

Truth carries conviction—sometimes. The clerk asked rather anxiously: "What's the trouble, sir?"

"I was in your hotel this evening, listening to the music; I might say that as I only intended to stay for a few minutes (I had missed an appointment in the lobby) I kept my coat and hat."

The clerk had learned more about his informant through this detail than if he had read a book about him; or so no doubt he thought.

"Just before the intermission ended," continued Gamadge, "a waiter opened a window in the dance room. I stepped out through it into the garden; I simply wished to find out whether it had stopped raining. It had, and I had the impulse to walk along through the place, smoking a cigarette."

The clerk knew all about those impulses. Had this old busybody come across a couple of unfortunates seeking privacy among the turned-up tables? By Heaven, you couldn't open a french window.

"There was no keep-out sign to prevent me," continued Gamadge. "I walked about, along the flagged paths. There is a dead man in your garden, sir."

After a moment the clerk made a sound of some kind. Gamadge plodded on:

"One of the musicians, I should judge. He was wearing a white coat. He was shot; there is a pistol beside him."

The clerk came to life: "Listen: who are you? I—"

Gamadge said coldly: "As I told you, I didn't care to wait through a police investigation. I am an elderly man, and tired. I will tell you the exact hour when I found him: thirty-eight minutes past eleven, and the band was playing."

The clerk shouted: "They're playing now!"

"You might count them."

Gamadge cut off an articulate cry from the clerk and left the booth. "I'm not elderly yet," he told himself, "but I'm tired all right; too tired to wait up several hours more doing Bishop's job for him."

He reached home, left his car in front of the house, let himself in, and a few minutes later fell into bed.

CHAPTER FIFTEEN

Perfection

GAMADGE SLEPT VERY late. Theodore, serving him his breakfast in the library, said that the telephone had been ringing a good deal.

"But I read your sign on my do', and I didn't answer."

"That's right. Never mind the newspapers yet, I'm not even going to look at them till my coffee begins to take hold."

It took hold while he was smoking his first cigarette, and he spread out the late city editions and glanced through them. Osterbridge had not made the front page, but city editors had decided, late as the news of his death had come in, that it was picturesque enough to catch the morning news:

***

CROONER SHOOTS SELF WHILE BAND PLAYS

***

There was no mention of Mrs. Tanner's party, of Bishop's conversation with Gamadge behind the scenes, of any anonymous telephone call to the management of the Stanton. A night watchman had discovered the body while on his regular rounds. Wayne Bishop, the band leader, had informed police that at the end of the intermission Osterbridge was not to be found, and that Miss Bean, singer for the outfit, had taken his place at the piano. Miss Bean supplied a little reader interest too: "Jack was such a nice boy, I wouldn't think he'd do anything like that. He must have had troubles we didn't know about." She had been very much overcome by the event, and in tears.

She, Bishop, and certain members of the orchestra had testified that Osterbridge had seemed worried during the evening.

Gamadge put down the papers and called up his friend Nordhall, Department of Homicide. Nordhall, unlike some of his colleagues, and after a trying initiation, had come to regard Gamadge's exploits as serviceable; he often showed his appreciation of them, in fact, by roaring with laughter.

He now greeted Gamadge buoyantly: "This is quite a coincidence. I've been trying to get you. Are you all dead up there?"

"Theodore and I are alone. I was asleep, and he must have been out."

Nordhall was amused. "I know. Hear you were at a party last night."

"That's so."

"They're all downtown making statements, all but Mrs. Tanner, who isn't so well. They want your statement too, of course, but you left before the shooting, I mean before the excitement, and you seem to have been dragged down to the Stanton by your friend Jennings, and I told them that being a friend of yours I'd interview you myself. So I let you have your sleep out. I've been busy."

"You won't regret that act of mercy, Nordhall."

"No, I was hoping you'd have something or other interesting to contribute. I didn't think you were down there just to listen to the band."

"Can I come down after lunch?"

"It is after lunch. After mine, anyway. Have you thrown your watch out of the window and decided to go by your own time from now on?"

Gamadge looked up at the old clock on the mantel.

"No wonder I feel so rested. How about my coming down now?"

"I have to go out again; see Mrs. Tanner. She's better, that friend of hers tells me. Collecting information on the state of mind of the deceased, you know," said Nordhall sepulchrally.

"Oh yes. He was worried."

"Was he? So they say. Be seeing you at four o'clock."

Gamadge put down the receiver, and then asked for the Welshes' suburban number. He got Sally Welsh on the wire.

"She got here all right, Mr. Gamadge."

"How's she getting along?"

"She seems to be fine. She's out in the yard sketching. I never saw anybody keep so busy. I looked at her picture, Mr. Gamadge, and she's left out the wash on the line. She says you're allowed to."

"What's she putting in?"

"I couldn't make out," said Sally laughing. "I didn't dare ask her."

"Better not, they hate that. I hope she's not too much trouble, Sally?"

"She's no trouble at all. Tom says it's like having a stuffed chipmunk in the place."

"Stuffed! Chipmunk, yes; stuffed, I shouldn't think so."

"She is like that when he's around."

"That's so, she'd be shy of the great hulk. Give her a message from me, will you, Sally? Tell her not to worry, I think her affairs are going to come out all right. And don't charge her much board, will you? I'll make it up to you. Charge her about half."

"That's what she offered me," said Sally, and joined in Gamadge's laughter. "But Tom's greatly impressed."

"By *her*?"

"At her being willing to come up here and stay with total strangers at your suggestion, when she doesn't know who you are. I mean she doesn't even know your name!"

"Well—er—we were a little hurried at the last. I told you it was an emergency."

"Tom nearly died laughing."

"In the circumstances I can't very well ask him to mind his own business. Regards to Miss Vesey, and say I'll keep in touch."

Gamadge spent the early afternoon reading his notes, making others, and thinking. At four o'clock he was in Nordhall's little office; Nordhall, a big blond man, leaned across his desk to shake hands. He was grinning.

"Sit down," he said. "Make yourself comfortable. Dying to make that statement, are you?"

"I want to see you about something else."

Nordhall looked at him, grinning no longer. "That so?"

"Let's hear about the suicide first."

"All right, let's see." Nordhall sorted papers on his desk. "We got the call at ten minutes past twelve. I was there about twelve-thirty. The newspapers didn't give it out, by the way, in fact they didn't have it then, but the management was tipped off by somebody telephoning in from a pay station. He said he'd stepped out in the garden and found the body at eleven-thirty-eight."

"That so?"

"Yes. Osterbridge had shot himself just under the right jawbone, and it would take his own mother to identify him from his face. But it's Osterbridge. Worried, was he? In a way I wouldn't blame him. The gun was a thirty-eight Colt automatic, and the bullets that killed Alice Dunbar came out of it."

Gamadge jerked upright in his chair.

Nordhall smiled at him, leaned back, and clasped his hands behind his head. "Neat, isn't it? He meets her at Mrs. Tanner's place in the Stanton—that's established. Mrs. Tanner told me so; poor thing, she's all upset about it. She'd entirely forgotten it, but she introduced them." He eyed Gamadge quizzically. "Might you have guessed that?"

"I thought it was possible," said Gamadge faintly.

"Don't let it get you, there's worse to come. Poor Mrs. Tanner, she was in bad shape; trembling like a leaf."

"Natural reaction from anxiety."

"What's that?" asked Nordhall sharply.

"Well, she'd be relieved to know that the case was closed, wouldn't she? Sister's murderer knows he'll be recognized by Miss Cole and Mrs. Flynn and he kills himself."

"Yes," said Nordhall, watching him. "It all turned on the finding of Alice Dunbar. He lived alone in a men's hotel, and he could easily have gone to and from the Scale house. And by the way, there never was any houseman; Fuller didn't have one. The local tradespeople say there wasn't a thing bought, no milk ordered, not a thing."

Gamadge nodded vaguely.

"I suppose that wouldn't come as much of a surprise to anybody. Would this surprise you? Macloud thinks the Dunbars did expect old Mrs. Woodworth's money; they thought Alice was going to get it."

"No, that wouldn't surprise me too much. There had to be money in the case somewhere."

"He says it's a hunch, but I wouldn't ignore a hunch of Mr. Macloud's, not for anything. Mrs. Tanner will admit it now. But when did Alice Dunbar get time off to meet Osterbridge at the Scale house? Well, how about the middle of the night?"

"There's that," agreed Gamadge, staring.

"Why not?"

"It's a mighty good idea, Nordhall."

"I don't know why you shouldn't have thought of it," said Nordhall modestly.

"You police are trained like that."

Nordhall gave him a suspicious glance, but his face was serious. He went on: "Unfortunately there isn't a print in the Fuller flat; guy must have lived in gloves; but of course he wasn't there much. Well, the thing explodes in his face yesterday—the body's found, Mrs. Tanner can connect him up with Alice Dunbar. No wonder he wanted to talk to her. He did, didn't he?"

"Certainly did."

"So," said Nordhall, sitting forward and putting his hands flat on the papers before him, "we have it all; all except his motive for killing that girl. Just because he's disappointed about the Woodworth money? Nonsense."

"Thin, yes."

"He might have had Mrs. Tanner as a second string, but we have no evidence of that. I wouldn't say she was interested in him at all." He added: "Not that way."

"Nor would I."

"That's where you come in handy, Gamadge; on the psychology."

"Thanks."

"But *we* get the information; we have the equipment for that." Nordhall smiled. "We've traced that Colt thirty-eight."

"What!"

"You know something?" Nordhall was grinning broadly. "I like giving you a shock now and then; instead of you bringing in the evidence and laying it down on the line the way that cat of yours would lay down a row of dead mice."

Gamadge said mechanically: "That metaphor is repulsive and the analogy is cock-eyed. My mice are never dead. I shouldn't have thought that gun could be traced, Nordhall."

"Not to Osterbridge?" Nordhall broke into laughter.

"Not to anybody."

"It was easy; we got it right away. It belonged to Richfield Tanner."

Gamadge sat silent, his hands on the arms of his chair. Looking up at last to meet Nordhall's triumphant gaze, he smiled.

"Like that, do you?"

"Yes." Gamadge felt for his cigarettes and got one into his mouth. He lighted it and spoke around it: "I like that very much."

"Mrs. Tanner didn't. She says she never laid eyes on it since before the war, when Tanner got his service forty-five. She can't imagine how Osterbridge ever got hold of it." Nordhall shifted papers around, looked up at Gamadge, and smiled. "Osterbridge didn't know Tanner, none of them knew him. He was never at the Stanton in his life, according to Mrs. Tanner, and so far as we can find out, Bishop didn't get near his outfit while they were both overseas; Bishop making that tour of camps, you know, and Dunbar was always with his staff, a thousand miles away from Tanner in the war."

Gamadge said, returning the smile: "We're getting a little away from Osterbridge."

"So we are. Mrs. Tanner says he might have picked up the gun in her suite, if he snooped around among her husband's things. But how she missed it if it was there, all these three years, she can't say. Would you think she'd be so thick with those types, Gamadge?"

"If she was bored, yes."

"Of course the gun lets her out, out of both murders, as killer or accessory. She wouldn't give that gun to anybody to murder anybody with. And you probably know that she never left her suite last night after you left her there; we have three witnesses, and the hotel maid and the house detective aren't lying, even if Mrs. Lynch would."

"I don't think she'd be likely to leave the suite, Nordhall."

"Besides which, she has a lot of alibi for the afternoon that her sister was killed. The whole Dunbar household, and then that cocktail party. She hadn't the time."

Gamadge was laughing. "What's become of the Osterbridge suicide, anyway?"

"Did you think he was a good candidate for the Fuller position?"

"Not very, no."

"Miss Cole describes him as the gigolo type, though."

"Why should Osterbridge go up there and disguise himself as his own character?"

"He wouldn't if he could help it. Is that why you went down to the Stanton, Gamadge? To look these people over?"

"I hadn't even heard of them. I went down to make Mrs. Tanner's acquaintance. I wondered whether Alice Dunbar might have met some of her sporting friends, that's all."

"Perhaps we're being too smart," said Nordhall, squinting at Gamadge thoughtfully. "But what a setup! Perfection. Osterbridge was worried, and wasn't that natural? He knew she'd be questioned again, now that Alice Dunbar's death was established; he wanted to brace her up, he had to be sure she wouldn't say he'd met her sister. He couldn't talk to her, so he goes out in the garden and shoots himself with a gun that nobody but a suicide would dare use—it can be traced. And he disfigures himself so badly that no jury would blame Miss Cole or Mrs. Flynn for not identifying him with Fuller. Even if they reconstructed him, nobody would blame anybody for failing to recognize him. So that takes care of that—he's Fuller. Perfect."

"He couldn't face Miss Cole and Mrs. Flynn, you mean."

"That's it. It's so good we ought to believe it. I have to hand it to that killer, I really do."

"He'd have to know how to get hold of Osterbridge."

"No trouble about that," said Nordhall gaily, "no trouble at all. You'd better have a look at the statement."

"Just a minute; I suppose Miss Cole and Mrs. Flynn haven't seen the others yet?"

Nordhall's gaiety faded. "They had a good look, while everybody was downtown making the statements and signing them; and nobody saw *them*. Neither of those women will swear to Bishop or Dunbar. Well, they're not the only people in the world; but that gun keeps it near home. Listen to some of these things here, they might amuse you."

"I'm in the mood."

CHAPTER SIXTEEN

Statements

"WE MIGHT GET rid of the small fry first." Nordhall picked up a carbon from the desk. "Your stooge, Mr. Jennings." He read aloud:

> Statement of Arthur Stone Jennings:
> Being an intimate friend of the Dunbar family, I wished to pay a call of condolence last night on Mrs. Richfield Tanner at the Stanton Hotel. I had informed Mrs. Tanner over the telephone that Mr. Henry Gamadge, a classmate of mine and a man of some literary standing, had seen Mr. Robert Macloud that afternoon. Mr. Macloud is a partner of Mr. Angus Dunbar's and an old friend of Mr. Gamadge's. Mrs. Tanner expressed a wish to see him and hear what later news about her sister's tragic death might have come in.

Nordhall looked up. "Sly dog. I mean you." He went on:

> We reached the Stanton at a little after nine, a few minutes late. The driving was very slow in the rain.

> We found Mrs. Tanner in a pitifully nervous condition, with a friend, Elinor Lynch, looking out for her. Some musical acquaintances dropped in, among them the singer Mr. Osterbridge. If he seemed worried, it was probably on Mrs. Tanner's account. He played the piano to divert her mind from her deep grief, but she soon gave up the effort to talk to us, and retired. I went home.

Nordhall's voice was now trembling a little. He replaced the statement in its folder, and raised his eyes to Gamadge's. They exchanged a solemn look.

Gamadge broke down first. His elbows on the desk, his head in his hands, he sat silent with his shoulders heaving. Nordhall rocked in his chair.

"Boy, what a hangover!" he gasped after a while. "And the Bean girl says there was enough liquor up there to drown her. Was there?"

"More. More."

"Was anybody sober at that wake?"

Gamadge, recovering himself, said that everybody else was. "And I think Mrs. Lynch was right; it was partly exhaustion and shock. After all, whether the sisters were congenial or not it would be a hideous shock, Nordhall."

"Did she say much before she retired? I'm glad you know one gentleman, Gamadge."

"Well, he went home."

"That's so. I suppose this Jennings couldn't have been the old peeker that telephoned the Stanton about finding Osterbridge in the garden? Sounds like him."

"Oh, Jennings wouldn't do a thing like that," said Gamadge hastily. "He'd never go wandering around like that, he's not the adventurous type at all."

"How about if we pinned the murder on him? He needn't have left then, there's no evidence when he left. He says he took a bus home."

"It's a wonderful idea," said Gamadge. "I like it as much as you do, but we mustn't get infatuated with it; he took a bus home because I let him down. If I hadn't, we'd have driven home in my car."

"Didn't he know you'd say so? That's when he planned it—when you wouldn't leave with him. Why look at it: he knew Alice Dunbar well, and what's more he knew Richfield Tanner and could have borrowed his gun. He wouldn't care if it was traced back to Mrs. Tanner—nobody was going to suspect *him*. He's alone in the city, alone in a brownstone house. Haven't I heard that he and his mother are hard up now, just manage to get by?"

"They're not well off, no," said Gamadge.

"He wanted that Woodworth money. When he knew she wasn't going to get it he had to get rid of her—she'd have denounced him to the Social Register."

"That's as good a motive as I've heard yet for that murder."

"Tell me a motive," said Nordhall, suddenly scowling.

"A killer like this one would have to have the best."

"He would; what is it?" Nordhall leaned back again. "Where were we before we began talking about Jennings? Oh yes. Did Mrs. Tanner say anything interesting before she passed out?"

"She thought the body you found couldn't be her sister's, because her sister wouldn't have bought or worn those things—like the red macintosh."

"We've got the dentist's report—it's Alice Dunbar all right, and as for the clothes she bought, she was just trying to look different." Nordhall shuffled through papers. "Here's the shopping list; everything's been traced back to three stores, ending with Stengel's."

He pushed the list towards Gamadge. "Hat, stockings, a white collar, a pair of 'costume' earrings, red raincoat, and make-up. Labels on some of the stuff, decipherable by experts because the raincoat was protection for it. The shopping bag—that's been traced too—protected her own things. They were all in it; her stockings and gloves, her hat, her handbag. Oh—the make-up was in the handbag. Nothing else in it but a handkerchief and some money—five dollars in small bills and change."

Gamadge looked down the list. He pushed it back at Nordhall. "I agree with you, she just wanted to look different."

Nordhall was reading another statement: "Here's Mrs. Lynch. Nothing much you wouldn't know already. She tells about Dunbar showing up and singing Osterbridge off the map. In the circumstances, would that show a certain amount of lack of human feeling?"

"Well, it was a breach of etiquette; he apologized afterwards for it. He wasn't known there, and"—Gamadge smiled—"it's a melancholy little song."

"O.K. Here's Miss Bean. You blew her to a snack in the supper room."

"Yes. She seems to be a grateful little thing," remarked Gamadge, looking amused.

"Doesn't like Mrs. Tanner. It looks as if she had to play gooseberry up in that suite. But apart from describing the party, and telling how she and Mrs. Lynch had to put the casualty to bed, she had no information. Oh—Osterbridge was worried because he felt all this sympathy for Mrs. Tanner.

"Dunbar says he got to the hotel around twenty to eleven—Mrs. Lynch corroborates. That right?"

"I should think so."

"Left just before the intermission. The only thing that looks funny at all about his doings last night is that he took a bus home too. I wouldn't have thought he cared for buses, especially buses on a rainy night. But he says there was a wait for a cab, and people getting their cars, and as it had stopped raining he just walked to Fifth. It would be a convenient way for him to get back to the Dunbars'. He has a key, nobody heard him come in."

Gamadge raised his eyebrows, and said nothing.

"It's how you look at it," continued Nordhall. "At that hour he could have slipped past the car lot without being noticed and gone into the garden. You know the way it's fixed there? The parked cars back up against a raised walk on that side, and the walk goes through an opening in a fence, through the garden and along the side of the hotel to another gate on the next block. And in a few minutes, if we believe Bishop, Osterbridge was out in front of a side door back there, smoking a cigarette. We did find one of his cigarettes there."

"Would Dunbar expect to find Osterbridge there?"

"That's it. That's why we go on to Mr. Bishop, who has a very interesting story to tell; it places him right on the spot, but then the bar he went to does the same, so perhaps it was just as well for him to be frank. He's frank, all right." Nordhall half-closed his eyes and looked at Gamadge narrowly. "What do you think of that personality?"

"He's wonderful."

"Isn't he, though? Mind you, we haven't a thing on either of those birds, not a thing. Well, his story is that he went out by that side door as soon as he got a raincoat on after the intermission started, and Osterbridge was standing on that raised walk smoking. The rain had stopped. They exchanged a few ordinary remarks; Bishop didn't notice anything wrong with him, and went off alone to this bar he patronizes on Lexington. Osterbridge wouldn't go."

"Did he usually go?"

"If he hadn't anything better to do, such as going up to entertain Mrs. Tanner."

"Who let that out?"

"Bean."

"I see."

"Well: Bishop says he came back about ten minutes before the end of the intermission, eleven-twenty. He looked around and couldn't find Osterbridge anywhere. The musicians and Miss Bean had been together in a sort of lounge they have back there, and they hadn't seen Osterbridge at all. Bishop told Miss Bean she'd have to play piano if he didn't show up. She went on stage to look over the music—that's right: she did. Bishop didn't know what to do or where to look. Never entered his head, he says, that Osterbridge would be outside in that wet garden, with all the chairs and tables upside down. He had to go on himself at eleven-thirty sharp. And that's his story."

"You say he got in and out by some gate there?"

"Yes, and the management's a little sore at him about leaving it ajar so he could get back in. The lock's fixed so you can't get at it to open it from outside. But Bishop showed us what he did about it, and though he calls it 'ajar' it was really not noticeably so from the street. You couldn't see that it wasn't shut. However, he won't be doing that anymore."

"It looks as though Osterbridge must have been killed soon after eleven, whether Bishop's telling the truth or not. *Would* he hang around long in that place?"

"So far as they can tell he was killed soon after eleven; anyway, he could have been. If Bishop didn't do it he just missed it. As for the shot being heard, if it was it wasn't noticed. There's a lot of horn blowing and backfiring and engines taking hold on both those streets at that time of the night, even in summer."

"Why should Bishop kill his best singer and piano player?"

"Only for the set-up. There's no other reason. He certainly wasn't jealous of him about Mrs. Tanner—even Bean admits she liked Bishop best. Why would she, Gamadge?"

"He was infinitely the more attractive of the two. More personality, more everything."

"Less hair. And he's a sick man—perhaps he's slipping."

"He can be attractive."

"He'd be a natural for a disguise. I never saw anybody so cool in my life. Take him or leave him—that's Mr. Wayne Bishop. He was right there in the garden at the right time, he didn't have to sneak past the car attendant or take a bus home. But his lawyer would say that anybody else could have got in there through either end of the place, both ends were open; and nobody says he ever met Alice Dunbar. Perhaps he's got reason to be cool. Know what I think? There'll never be a conviction for either of those murders."

Gamadge, his elbow on Nordhall's desk, was playing with the lid of the corroded inkstand. He said: "Perhaps not."

Nordhall slammed his papers together and shot them into the folder. Suddenly he looked up. "I was forgetting all about you."

"Were you? I didn't notice it. No hard feelings."

"I mean why did you want to see me? Didn't you say it wasn't about this case?"

"Not directly. I'm afraid it will sound rather an anticlimax, after all your fireworks."

"Never mind, you're always interesting," said Nordhall. "Let's have it."

"Just an idea of mine. I thought you might help me out on it."

"Go ahead, what is it?"

"Well, perhaps you remember that Alice Dunbar was an artist?"

CHAPTER SEVENTEEN

Black Valentine

NORDHALL LOOKED ASTONISHED at this introduction of new material. "She was if you say so."

"Surely you remember that she used to design gift cards for her friends?"

"It slipped my mind."

"She used to work at it down at her art teacher's studio—woman who taught her from the time she was in school."

"I'm beginning to remember something about it. The teacher was up in Vermont or somewhere with a class, and Missing Persons and the newspapers got in touch with her, trying to find out if Alice Dunbar had gone there or written."

"Some of the papers made a feature of the gift-card business, it helped with the background of the case. I had an idea that a lot of that work—designs and so on—might still be in the studio. Miss Bransome was the name, wasn't it?"

Nordhall sat chewing his lip and looking blank.

"And if there's any finished work," continued Gamadge, "and there might be—she'd do some of it a long time beforehand, months ahead—she'd letter the cards herself."

Intelligence was beginning to take the place of the blankness in Nordhall's eyes: "You mean messages?"

"Each card was different, I suppose; she wouldn't send them out to a printer. She'd do the lettering for each in some appropriate way, perhaps; Old English script, Gothic letters. It's just an idea."

"I get it."

"If she was in love with this Fuller, might there be some hint of it on a card? Even a name?"

Nordhall pushed out his lower lip. "She seems to have been mighty careful not to leave any evidence against him."

"But nobody'd see the cards; the art teacher wouldn't even be interested in them, apart from the cover designs. If she'd found anything, she'd have produced it long ago."

"You want me to get in touch with her?" Nordhall was still puzzled, and sceptical.

"I meant to have a look myself, but of course I wouldn't dream of touching the things without at least two witnesses, both of them policemen."

"Well, we can call her."

"She's still away. I got her address, forwarding address, and I—er—wrote to her. She seems very nice; she sent me her keys."

Nordhall sank back in his chair. "She sends her keys to a total stranger because he asks for them, and gives him permission to dig around in her apartment?"

"Well, she's as anxious as we are to get at the bottom of this mystery, Nordhall; old pupil and all. I gave her references. And I don't suppose there's much in her place that we'd want to lug away with us; she'd have her valuables with her or in storage."

"Where is she?"

"Up in Westchester. She doesn't feel like coming into town herself, the hot weather gets her." Gamadge added: "She can't be young."

"So you want me to take the sergeant and go down with you and look through those cards?" Nordhall was gazing at Gamadge earnestly. "This is a very goody-goody streak you've developed, Bud. I'd have expected you to go down there yourself, and break into the place, and come back with Alice Dunbar's boyfriend's name in the bag."

"Sorry I've impressed you as a complete crackbrain. I know when I need a witness."

"When do you want to go?"

"I thought this evening."

"Can't do. I'm too busy."

Gamadge was playing with the lid of the inkstand, snapping it up and down. He said: "I rather wondered whether this Fuller mightn't have had the same idea that I had."

"You what?" asked Nordhall.

"Why shouldn't he? Don't you think that the discovery of the body has alerted him to danger as he wasn't alerted before? He'll think of everything. But until this evening he won't have had a chance to get in there and look those cards over."

Nordhall sat back and began to smile.

"Miss Bransome's away," continued Gamadge gently. "'There's a sign on her mailbox that says so. But this evening I could take the sign off. He wouldn't go there in the daytime."

"He wouldn't go there at all," said Nordhall with assumed patience. "He'd be giving himself away. Or do you think he'll go in there shooting, perhaps? Just to get a look at those cards?"

"Would Fuller mind doing that?"

"He'd mind putting the spotlight on himself," said Nordhall, aggravated. "Osterbridge—"

"Have you officially written Osterbridge off as a suicide?"

"No. But—"

"Have you arrested Dunbar or Bishop or held them for questioning?"

"No, it's too soon."

"I can tell you just when he'll get to the studio building, Nordhall," said Gamadge; he relinquished the lid of the inkstand, looked at his stained finger, rubbed it on Nordhall's blotter, and went on in a tone that seemed almost to lack interest. "Not by daylight; that, as you imply, wouldn't do. Not too late—Miss Bransome is alone in that building after five, and she wouldn't be likely to click that door switch after nine o'clock at night. I'd say about eight. Couldn't you make it? By dark, perhaps? I'd go down first and let you in."

"Why first?" asked Nordhall.

"Well, he might come a little early. I couldn't bear to miss him."

"Now don't put yourself out in front, Gamadge," said Nordhall with pretended anxiety. "We'd miss you."

"I wouldn't let him in till you came; but I might get a look at him from the windows as he came and went."

Nordhall was reduced to silence. He sat thinking, his face a study in doubt.

"This party," said Gamadge, "has supreme self-confidence. What happens when such a character suddenly finds his props knocked out from under him? The shock alone would do for him."

"Think so? And how much good will a confession in those circumstances do us?"

"If he pulled a gun you could arrest him, anyway. Don't you even want to know who Fuller is, Nordhall?"

Nordhall laughed. "All right, I'll be there with the sergeant at half past seven. But I won't wait all night."

Gamadge rose. "Here's the address. I'm awfully sorry, Nordhall, but I have to break it to you that the elevator won't be running. It's only four flights up, though."

"That's nothing," said Nordhall jovially. "May kill the sergeant, but Murphy isn't the only one; and what's a few lives in a big experiment?"

"Then that's settled."

"Quite a scoop for us," said Nordhall, laughing.

"I'll work out a plan of campaign and submit it when you get there."

"I bet you will."

Gamadge went home and asked for high tea. Theodore

served him reluctantly with sandwiches, salad, and coffee, and he had a couple of drinks. At six-fifteen he started on foot for the Bransome place.

Feeling as though he were performing an act of doom, he removed the sign from her bell. He let himself into the dark hallway, climbed the dark flight of stairs, switched on the light at the head of the last flight, and picked up Miss Bransome's clean and empty garbage can. He let himself into the flat and shut the door after him.

He put on lights, took the garbage can into the front room and shoved it into the cupboard under the wall-kitchen. Walking back through the passage he hesitated, stopped, returned to the living-room, and picked up two small felt rugs. He carried them into the passage and laid them end to end between the studio door and the bathroom. There was already a rug inside the studio doorway, extending as far as the end of the work-table. He straightened it.

Lamp on in the living-room, lamp on in the studio; all shades well down. He brought a wicker chair with a cushion in it to the end of the work-table nearest the door, placed another chair at the table, shoved other chairs and the painting stool to the other side of the room. Then he went over to the cupboard which Miss Bransome had indicated, and opened it.

It was full of artists' materials, from charcoal sticks and chalks to tubes of oil paint, bottles of turpentine, stretched canvases, and big portfolios of Whatman paper. But one shelf had been devoted to Alice Dunbar. There was a large open box of her cards and designs, there were tracing paper, Indian ink, fine pens, and pencils; there was a flat tin full of pans of water-colour; there were an agate burnisher, and a tray full of little pieces of white blotting paper cut into sharp-cornered squares and diamonds.

Gamadge took out the box of cards, put it on the work-table, sat down, and began to sort through its contents. Charming things he found; little snow scenes for Christmas cards; illuminated oblongs like pages from a Book of Hours, all bright colours and burnished gold; small clusters and bouquets of flowers in watercolour. There were two lace-paper cards that must be intended for valentines. One was a pinkish mauve with a delicate little cluster of flowers on it and no greeting inside; the other had more brilliant flowers, against a black background, with verses in Gothic lettering.

Gamadge sat with his head in his hands reading the black valentine; five short lines of interior poetry. The doorbell went off like a fire alarm, startling him half out of his senses. He recovered himself, glanced at the daylight still showing at the edges of the window shades, and said: "Can't be." But his mouth felt dry as he got up and clicked the switch that opened the front door.

The visitor took a long time to climb the stairs; he waited, standing just inside the door, listened with relief to the sound of footsteps, opened the door as soon as the bell rang.

Abigail Tanner stood there, looking at him almost without surprise—as if anything could happen in the dream world she inhabited now. Her face was pale and swollen, not made up at all. She was wearing a plain black dress, thin black stockings, white gloves, and a little black hat with a veil.

He said: "Come in, Mrs. Tanner. Miss Bransome isn't in. Can I do something for you?"

She asked in a halting, roughened voice: "What are you doing here?"

"I came to look at your sister's gift cards. Didn't you?"

He stood aside, and she went past him into the studio. But he was close behind her when she put out her hand to the black valentine; his own closed over hers.

"You know I can't let you have that, Mrs. Tanner."

She drew her hand away. He picked up the valentine and opened it. "Will you read it? Not very good verse, but her style was cramped by the restrictions of the form."

Will you be my valentine?
Always constant, always mine?

You to me as I to you,
Never wandering
Ever true.

Mrs. Tanner stood staring at the lines.

"No name on it, you see," said Gamadge. "That's all there is."

She burst out crying. "I wanted to tear it up."

"You like him, don't you?"

"That's all over. He must have met her behind my back. He only laughs. He says they can't do anything, but they're following him everywhere. If I only knew how he ever got hold of Richie's gun! That makes it all so senseless that I feel as if none of it could be true."

"It was a sporting try of yours."

She put the handkerchief away that she had been wiping her eyes with. "I never should have known such people. You can't tell what they'll do. But I couldn't believe—until they told me this morning about Jack Osterbridge."

"You didn't agree with the suicide theory, then?"

"Jack Osterbridge! It's despicable to put it all on him. But that's what they do—turn on their friends. What if Alice did meet Jack in my suite once? She hardly noticed him."

"You told the police that, I suppose?"

"Yes, I did. I never thought..." She paused, and added wildly: "I know he needs money. Alice must have told him she was expecting Great-aunt Woodworth's."

"Bishop's really a gambler?"

"Of course he is." She turned away. "I suppose they'll never believe now that I didn't know he'd met Alice. Well, *she* found him out!"

"Mrs. Tanner, if I were you I'd go back to my family. I'd go now."

"I'm going. Nellie Lynch will send me my clothes. I'm going now. I never want to see the Stanton again."

"Better not, perhaps."

"My father and mother will be furious with me; they'll never forgive me for introducing Jack Osterbridge to Alice; but at least I needn't be involved myself. That"—she looked at the black valentine—"won't matter much. Just one more thing."

She went out into the hall. Gamadge opened the door for her, and stood on the landing until she had gone down the stairs and out of the building; he heard the front door close behind her.

He went back, sat down again, and continued to search through rough sketches and designs for greeting cards. When the doorbell rang again he was prepared for it—his watch said twenty-eight minutes past seven.

He got up, went into the passage, and clicked the switch. Footsteps began to climb the stairs, lumbering.

CHAPTER EIGHTEEN

Position Is Everything

NORDHALL AND SERGEANT Murphy came into the flat very much as Gamadge's cat Martin would have come into it for the first time—warily, curiously, with an indefinable air of scepticism. Nordhall followed Gamadge into the studio; the sergeant, methodically and as a matter of routine, plodded to and fro looking into rooms and closets, opening and shutting doors.

Nordhall's eye fell on the scattered gift cards. "Couldn't wait for your witnesses after all. I don't think you meant me to put much stock in all that, did you? I mean you didn't expect to actually find anything."

"Well, as a matter of fact I did find something." Gamadge held out the black valentine. "Poetry in it."

Nordhall looked at him, looked at the bright flowers on the cover, opened the valentine, and ran his eye over the verse. The sergeant came in, and glanced over Nordhall's shoulder; his expression was one of intelligent interest, his lips formed words. At last he spoke aloud: "Just a valentine. They're supposed to be a secret, they don't give any names."

"Only the addressee's. Read the first letters downward, Sergeant," said Gamadge.

"...I'll be—"

Nordhall said reflectively: "Gives us what we want, I imagine."

"You couldn't convict on it."

"No. Big help, though."

Gamadge asked: "May I borrow it back?" He took it from Nordhall. "I admit I haven't found any more acrostics yet."

"No, I guess that was special."

"You just missed a caller, Nordhall."

Nordhall's head jerked up. Gamadge laughed. "No, Fuller didn't come; but when the doorbell rang and I had to click that switch I was scared silly. I'm afraid of Mr. Fuller."

"So you clicked the switch." Nordhall fixed him with a pale, amused stare.

"Yes, it was too early. It was Abigail Tanner."

"No! Looking for that?" Nordhall jerked his head at the valentine.

"Yes. You know what I think, Nordhall? I think she commissioned it. I think she got her sister to do it for her; as a kind of joke, I suppose. It would be a quaint thing for Abigail Tanner to send Wayne Bishop."

"I don't get that," said Nordhall.

Gamadge looked down at it. "I wonder what she bought it with? A little party at the Stanton, a glimpse of the gay life?"

"What's the argument?" insisted Nordhall impatiently.

"Why should she come here, involving herself further in a case she wants to get clear of, to destroy evidence that her sister knew Wayne Bishop? She's sure he's Fuller. But if this thing was done for her to send him, she might not know exactly what was in it; her own name might have been worked in somewhere—evidently she hadn't seen it yet."

The sergeant observed: "Valentine's Day is six months off."

"These things take a long time to do properly—that lettering is a work of art, spaced and all; beautiful script. The picture is beautifully done. She might have wanted to get it off her hands before she tackled Christmas cards, birthday cards."

"Mrs. Tanner wouldn't destroy evidence against Bishop?" asked Nordhall. "She was fond of him; they all say so."

"There's no proof of it but hearsay, and she isn't fond of him now. I'll tell you what I think happened to Mrs. Tanner," said Gamadge, laying the valentine down on the work-table and lighting a cigarette. "She thought up to yesterday that her sister had simply gone away; and if she thought that, there must have been plenty of reason for her thinking so. But yesterday her sister's body was found; Alice Dunbar had been murdered and brutally huddled away underground; and the murderer had lived in sight of the grave for a week afterwards. Mrs. Tanner couldn't help thinking of Bishop; he might have introduced himself to Alice at the Stanton—she thinks he did, 'behind her back.' He's a gambler and needs money. And most of all, he's an enigma to her; a man so entirely out of her experience that she thinks he might be capable of anything. That's what attracted her to him, you know—he was the nearest thing to romantic danger that she had ever had a chance to know. Never mind Richfield Tanner's tough friends—they weren't a bit like Wayne Bishop."

"I guess that's so," said Nordhall grimly.

"So she thought of him, and she thought of this commissioned valentine. She fought the thing hard; she collapsed fighting it. Today she heard about Osterbridge's alleged suicide, and she gave up. Bishop had had opportunity, and she felt as we did about the motive for this second murder. What did she think of her valentine then? She *must* get hold of it. Could she go down in criminal history as the woman who sent Bishop that?"

"So she comes here and finds her name isn't on it, and that lets her out," said the sergeant.

"And perhaps it catches the murderer," said Nordhall, "who hadn't been doing the right thing by her anyway."

"So he comes here to get it himself," said the sergeant.

"Or whatever Alice Dunbar was getting ready for him. I suppose Mrs. Tanner couldn't help telling him something about it." Nordhall looked around him. "He ought to be coming along pretty soon, if he's coming; but did you think he'd be coming alone?"

"He could get in here, Nordhall; they wouldn't expect him to come here. Or did you say anything?"

"Well, no, I didn't."

Gamadge smiled at the sergeant. "Boss doesn't take me seriously, Sergeant."

"He does, Mr. Gamadge," said the sergeant earnestly, "it's just that he didn't take these Christmas cards serious."

Nordhall bit his lip in perplexity. "It makes some kind of sense, I'll say that. Well, he comes here; I won't say he might not manage it—steps into the vestibule in the dark, and then you open the door and he's in. Say he does it. What happens?"

"You couldn't do a thing to him unless he misbehaved himself, Nordhall."

"That's so."

"Well, I fixed this chair for him here at the end of the table with his back to the passage. If you and the sergeant were in the bathroom, say, it's only a step from this, and the door opens right—I'd sit in this chair and talk to him."

"Fine," said Nordhall with a blank look.

"Just a frank talk," continued Gamadge. "It might upset him. But before he could do anything about it you'd both be on top of him—wouldn't you?"

"Well, I hope so. But we might be a little late," said Nordhall, "and you're scared of Fuller."

"We'd be ready for him."

"What makes you think he'd sit down in the right chair?"

"If he tries to throw me out of mine you can arrest him for assault. I'll bring charges," said Gamadge. "And you'll find he has a gun on him, and that'll make it even simpler."

"So at least we have him in the coop, with some explaining to do. It can't hurt us to try it," said Nordhall, "and I must say I'd like to hear that frank talk. I'd hate to miss that."

"Oh, it's a beauty," Gamadge assured him.

They looked at each other. "He might be really tough," said Nordhall. "If he's Fuller, he's as tough as they come."

"Don't remind me."

The bell rang; it had its usual first effect on the two

policemen, who jerked round in unison. "All the way downstairs," said Gamadge kindly. "No cause for alarm. Now if you'll just…"

A few seconds later he was alone in the passage. He clicked the switch. "I'll put out the light here," he said, "or at least unscrew the bulb a little. Not a sound out of either of you, now, unless he starts to pull a gun. Have you a good view?"

"Perfect," said Nordhall. "And don't give me any more orders."

Steps mounted the stairs. Gamadge went back into the studio, and waited. When the doorbell rang he walked the few feet necessary, and swung the door open. He stared, and laughed.

"I expected somebody else," he said. "I'm afraid you've spoiled a party, Mr. Dunbar."

Bruce Dunbar stood with his hat pushed back on his head and a light overcoat on his arm. He stared back, and smiled. "Party?"

"I'll tell you. Come in."

Dunbar came into the passage, glancing around him. "I was looking for Miss Bransome—the art teacher, you know. Alice's art teacher." He took off his hat and gloves, looked around him again.

"She stepped out."

"You're Mr. Gamadge, aren't you?" Dunbar surveyed him with curiosity and interest. "We met last night."

"That's so. And *I* met your cousin and some other people; I got some notions afterwards, crazy perhaps, but I wondered whether I mightn't verify them here. I'll explain."

Dunbar said: "I got some notions myself. I happened to remember this art teacher—or rather, I was looking back over old newspapers at the Dunbar house, and I came across her. Nobody seems to have bothered much with Miss Bransome. I thought I'd like a little talk with her about my cousin Alice. She might just remember something." He came farther into the passage, and Gamadge closed the door. "You have the same idea?" he asked, puzzled.

"Yes. I'll explain if you'll come into the studio."

Dunbar followed him through the doorway, laid his coat and

hat on the work-table, and sat down with commendable docility in the nearest chair; Gamadge had already pulled out the other one to half-face him.

"So this is where she did her painting," said Dunbar, his eyes moving from object to object about the room. "Rather nice place, too."

Gamadge offered him a cigarette. He accepted it absent-mindedly.

"You know, Mr. Dunbar," said Gamadge, smiling a little, "I think you must be as sceptical of that Osterbridge suicide as the rest of them are."

Dunbar returned his smile. "Well, they've turned me loose. I'm on my way to Washington, I have a translating job on hand for my old chief in Counter-Intelligence, and I'm glad to be able to get back before the weekend. But it doesn't matter what train I take this evening. I assumed that they—police, I mean—swallowed the Osterbridge suicide whole."

"They're chewing on it yet, I think. Otherwise they'd have arrested Bishop. I'll tell you my notion, Mr. Dunbar. I happened to think of the gift cards Alice Dunbar painted."

"Gift cards?" Dunbar's astonishment was as genuine as his start of surprise.

"I couldn't help wondering whether there were any personal messages or greetings on any of them."

Dunbar followed his glance, down to the scattered cards on the table. "I'll be darned! Never thought of them."

"It was a long shot." Gamadge pushed the black valentine towards him. "Look at this."

Dunbar picked it up, looked at the cover, turned it back, and frowned over the verse within. After a minute he raised his eyes, the light of amazement in them. "And I didn't know she'd ever laid eyes on him! Will this do the trick, should you say?"

"It might get him arrested. It couldn't convict him."

"But damn it all, she did cards for me—I think she was doing one—an illuminated Christmas thing. Wait a minute." He leaned forward and pushed bright squares and oblongs around. "Here, this is it." He studied it rather gravely, passed it rather sadly to Gamadge. It was a pretty burnished page, unfolded; red and blue flowers, stars, butterflies. A blank space in the middle not much bigger than a postage stamp. "She liked butterflies for all seasons."

Gamadge said: "Nobody would pay much attention to anything she did for you—a relative." He laid the card down. "But Bishop!"

"That's so." Dunbar sat back, frowning and smoking. "I should say it might do for him."

"Well, they'd still have a little trouble about it. I don't see myself how Bishop could possibly get into another character; up at the Woodworth place, I mean. Bishop is himself; after I met him last night in Mrs. Tanner's room I had a hard time thinking of him in an assumed personality. But that's just my opinion."

"I only had a look at him on the stage; it might be mine, if I thought about it," agreed Dunbar.

"And then he did put himself on the spot, you know; it was rash of him to kill Osterbridge in a place that wasn't freely accessible to anybody but himself. He could have walked home with him and shot him in a dark street. But there's always the double-bluff, unfortunately."

"There is. I can see that."

"And suppose Mrs. Tanner wanted to save him, and was willing to swear on oath that that card had been done for him at her request?"

"My God, would Abigail do that?" He looked deeply distressed. "Hanged if I know what's got into her since Richie died."

"And they can't connect Bishop and the gun."

"That's the damnedest puzzle of all."

"I don't think so," said Gamadge. "The puzzle is why Bishop should have killed Alice Dunbar. But I have an answer to it."

"You have?" Dunbar's interest was faint.

"If you'll sit on the party, Mr. Dunbar," said Gamadge, smiling at him, "I'll tell you the answer."

"But what is the party?"

Gamadge put his finger on the black valentine. "Bishop's no fool. Won't he think of this—if I did?"

"You mean he'll come here?" Dunbar straightened in his chair.

"It's the first chance he's had since your cousin's body was found. Miss Bransome has been away. There was a sign that said so on her mailbox. It's off now."

"Yes, I thought she was here."

"He may be followed, but I wouldn't put it past Bishop to slip in."

Dunbar was leaning forward, lips parted. "Then we'd know!" He slowly shook his head. "Another long shot, isn't it?"

"I'll tell you how long a shot I think it is." Gamadge pulled Miss Bransome's pottery bowl towards him and shook off the ash of his cigarette into it. "I asked Miss Bransome to spend the evening with friends, and I sent for police. There'll be plain-clothes men down below."

"We'll get shot first," said Dunbar, laughing.

"Not if we aren't in view. We'll see what he does, though. Pretty soon he'll have his after-dinner interval—if he's still leading the band. I suppose he is. He might even be playing piano for them—Mrs. Lynch said he could do anything."

Dunbar said after a moment: "I never saw such a fellow as you are. You'd persuade anybody of anything. What on earth is your interest in it, for Heaven's sake?"

"I'm a jelly of sentiment. I hate to think of Osterbridge's family and friends—bracing themselves for a criminal's obsequies and following him to a suicide's grave, when he hasn't done anything but play the piano well and sing annoyingly."

"I rather hate it too."

"You're really staying? I'd like another witness."

"Of course I am."

"Then," said Gamadge, leaning back as if relaxed in his chair, "I'll tell you why Bishop killed Alice Dunbar."

CHAPTER NINETEEN

Red Raincoat

"YOU CAN HELP me set the stage for this drama," said Gamadge, settling back and crossing his knees. "You knew Alice Dunbar and I didn't. I gather that she was a quiet type, repressed and lonely?"

"More than that," said Dunbar. He was sitting back too, his elbow on the table, his other hand, with a cigarette in it, resting on the table's edge. His thinnish face was still sceptical, but it showed more interest. "She was a disappointed woman; thwarted, you know. Ever since her engagement was broken—I didn't know her then, but Gail told me—she hadn't shown any spirit at all. I hate the jargon, but don't they call it frustrated?"

Gamadge said: "I'd go farther. I'd say that that dressing up and running away shows something like madness in a type like hers; I'd say she was over the edge."

"Well, it looked so."

"The bitterness of a poisoned heart. Let's go back to her first acquaintance with Mr. Fuller. She fell in love again, and it seemed to be reciprocal; what it must have meant to her! Everything: happiness, freedom, the sense of being important to someone she cared about, of having a place again in a living world. But Mr. Fuller warned her—he wouldn't subject her to a life of comparative poverty, he was too generous a soul for that. They'd wait until they were sure of the Woodworth money. Until then, not a word to anyone; they could meet somewhere, he'd find a place."

"Wait a minute, wait a minute," said Dunbar. "Woodworth money? What money? She wasn't getting that."

"She thought she was. All the Dunbars thought she was, and Mr. Fuller was counting on it. It's a fact, Mr. Dunbar; Abigail Tanner admits it."

"I'll be jiggered."

"But Fuller was a very cagey man, and he never counted on anything until it was in his hand. These gamblers—they hope, but they know enough not to count on the cash till the ball stops rolling. So, quite unknown to Alice Dunbar, he went up to the Woodworth place in September, put on a very good show as a freelance landscape gardener, interested the old lady—she was used to entertaining young men by that time—and did some fishing. Mrs. Woodworth didn't tell him her financial arrangements, he got no information about her will; but all the same he killed her."

Dunbar jerked upright in his chair. "Is that a fact?"

"No, we touch on fantasy there. Few doubt it now. He shoved her down a long flight of stairs, and she had a shock and her second stroke and died. If she had fallen herself, the result would have been the same.

"She had given Fuller a reference to Mr. Scale, her old friend, and he had established himself in the Scale apartment. He was of course seldom there, but he managed to meet Alice Dunbar there somehow—the police suggest the middle of the night."

Dunbar raised his eyebrows and tapped the table with his free hand.

"Think," said Gamadge, "what he had come to mean to her. And by the end of that week, she knew she wasn't going to get the Woodworth million. He knew it too, through her or through the newspapers; but he had an engagement with her at the Scale apartment on the following Friday afternoon, and he judged it wise to be there. He had to be there. He was used, perhaps, to dealing with broken hearts, and he was good at it; he could remind her of their bargain, and he could send her away comforted with those touching assurances of undying love and regret that keep broken hearts from flying to pieces and littering up the whole landscape.

"But he knew *something* about Alice Dunbar; more than anyone else knew; what he had meant to her, what a long and empty life without him would mean to her. She might kill herself, it was possible. Didn't she have that gun that Richfield Tanner gave her when he went to the war?"

Dunbar said sharply: "I didn't know he'd given it to her."

"She was a romantic, and he was kind to his sister-in-law. If she asked for it as a characteristic reminder of a fighting man, he'd let her have it. He had his own service gun. Doesn't that solve the mystery of the Tanner thirty-eight?"

Dunbar said slowly: "It does, I suppose."

"So Mr. Fuller," continued Gamadge, "not wanting to run the risk of leaving her dead body on the Scale premises (we know now what kind of risk it would have been), dug a grave."

Dunbar raised his eyes. "You're ingenious."

"No; logical. He dug a grave, and when she came he was ready for her; he'd prevent tragedy if he could. But even Fuller didn't quite understand the bitterness of that poisoned heart. Alice Dunbar wasn't going to lose another man to any other woman; she wasn't intending to kill herself if he abandoned her—she was going to kill him. He realized it just in time."

Dunbar said with a half laugh: "Fantastic."

"Certainly not; there's good evidence. But first let's dispose of the big scene: the Tanner gun is pointed at Mr. Fuller, but he's a man who thinks fast, and as I said, he was ready for her. She'd never killed anyone before, you know—she wasn't an expert, and perhaps she didn't really want to kill him. He got hold of the gun, and he got her arm behind her back." Gamadge lighted a cigarette and looked at it. "Would you say that the rest of the scene was an accident?"

"In your drama," said Dunbar, after a pause, "it couldn't be an accident."

"Not very well. He buried her, and he thought her body would never be found. Wasn't that a curious thing, the way it was found?"

Dunbar said slowly: "I suppose it was. I hadn't thought about it."

"I mean a stranger dropping in looking for a flat, and then fading out forever?"

"People don't want to be mixed up in a murder case. You could try it sometime," said Dunbar, with a faint smile.

"Still, it was odd. Very odd. He must have been a dowser who finds graves. Well, the body was found, and so Mr. Osterbridge was murdered to give us a killer and close up the case."

Gamadge lapsed into silence. Dunbar said at last: "It sounds a little flimsy without some of that evidence you mentioned."

"Oh yes," said Gamadge, with a start. "I forgot. It's that disguise she was wearing."

"You mean the red raincoat and everything?" asked Dunbar with surprise.

"And everything. As Mrs. Tanner said last night, she wanted to look different; but would a woman going to meet a man she loved and run off with him, would a woman even planning only to run off, dress herself up in a cheap and nasty way? If she'd planned the elopement she could have saved up and got herself better things to wear; if it was a spur-of-the-moment thing, she could still have found decent quiet things, things that wouldn't startle a man out of his wits, things that wouldn't make her a sight."

Dunbar reflected, his fingers playing with the gift cards. "She wanted to be out of character," he said at last. "An entirely different type."

"Mr. Dunbar," said Gamadge, his eyes on the other's frowning face, "why does a man or a woman put on that kind of disguise—the kind of disguise that changes them so basically they simply can't be recognized? Why did Fuller, up at the Woodworth place? They don't do it for keeps—for the fun of it. They do it as a temporary precaution when they're going to commit a crime."

Dunbar looked up. He said: "That's pure conjecture."

"Is it? Then what became of her gloves?"

"Gloves?"

"Did you see a list of what she was wearing when she was found, and what was in that shopping bag?"

"Yes, they had one at the house, I—"

"All her own things she put into that big paper bag, because she wanted to keep them; they cost money, she was on an allowance; she wasn't going to throw them away: her stockings, her hat, her handbag—the large bag she carried the gun in, you know—her gloves.

"She didn't wear gloves in that grave, and none have been found. If they'd been found they'd have been listed."

"Nonsense; she simply didn't buy gloves."

"Alice Dunbar didn't buy gloves? They're a second skin to people like Alice Dunbar, and if she could have imagined herself without them, she'd have imagined herself without stockings and a hat, bought a cotton scarf and saved money. Now why have those gloves disappeared? Because they had gun-grease on them, perhaps powder too?"

Dunbar said nothing.

"Of course she wore them," added Gamadge, crushing out his half-smoked cigarette, "because she wasn't going to leave prints in the Scale apartment. I mean she didn't take them off there. And I swear I don't think Fuller ever took his off either, except to wash his hands. Not that afternoon, anyhow. Handled each other with gloves, didn't they? Poison to each other from the day they met. Well, they came of the same stock."

Gamadge had the feeling that Dunbar was looking at him with bright eyes through a clay-coloured mask.

"And now, Mr. Dunbar," he said, "shall I tell you the real reason why you came to see Miss Bransome this evening?" He leaned forward across the corner of the table. "Why I sent her away? Why I got police?"

Dunbar's face did not change, but his hand disappeared under the fold of the topcoat on the table, his shoulders stiffened.

"What will that get you?" asked Gamadge gently. "The police are there now."

"I'll take a chance on them," said Dunbar, and his voice cracked. He had his big gun half-way out of the topcoat when Nordhall's hand came down on his wrist; two seconds later the sergeant had his other arm in a double grip—he was unable to move either hand an inch. He didn't need to. Gamadge saw the grey mask change, wrenched into the semblance of another—the insane mask of Greek tragedy; then he ducked his head down as if listening, and pulled the trigger of his gun.

It sounded like a cannon, even through the cloth of the coat. Gamadge was on his feet; the three stood gazing down at the visible half of Dunbar's face, no longer recognizable as a face, as anything. There was a silence that seemed absolute.

The sergeant broke it: "You got them across so fast he couldn't take care of them. He thinks quick, but I'd say he was somebody that died of fright."

Nordhall wasn't philosophizing. He said with realistic calm: "We're going to catch hell for this."

"Why?" Gamadge was propped against the side of the table. "You couldn't do anything till he started to pull the gun."

Nordhall was leaning over. "His service forty-five."

The sergeant had moved back a little. "Messed himself up worse than Osterbridge." His eyes went in bewilderment to the gift cards, and what remained in the cardboard box: "There's got to be something on one of those things, to break him down that way. But I could have swore he was surprised when you mentioned them. But there's got to be something."

Nordhall stood up and took his hand off Dunbar's wrist. He asked: "Where's the telephone?"

"Front room," said Gamadge. "I want a drink."

Nordhall met his eyes. "You do at that. Go ahead, beat it, but be on hand by the time the big shots get here, or I'll be in real trouble, and you too."

"There's one waiting for me not far off."

Gamadge leapt down the flights of stairs, and hurried to the nearest bar. He had his drink, and then sought the telephone. He called the Welsh number; Miss Bransome answered.

"Hello, Miss Bransome, know my name now?"

"Mr. Gamadge. What—"

"It's all right, and it's all over. You can come home tomorrow. I wouldn't advise tonight, they'll be mopping up in your place until late."

"Mop... You caught him?"

"The police did."

"Who was it? Who was it?"

"I'm not allowed to say. You'll see it in the paper. They may call you tonight, it's possible; so I got in ahead of them. Not a word about me, you understand, and not too many words about anything else. They think he came to your place to look at those cards Alice Dunbar painted. Gift cards."

"I never thought of them from the day last spring she put them away for the summer. What—"

"They'll tell you all about it. It's just your bad luck that he wanted a look at them and came and killed himself in your flat. But you'll never know it by the looks of the place when you get back—unless they go smearing everything with fingerprint powder."

"Mr. Gamadge... I can't even say it. I don't know how. I—"

"No words needed, Miss Bransome. I'll consider them all said. Good night."

He hastened back, and was considerably disgusted at

having to argue himself in, past uniforms. But the elevator was now working in its own erratic way, and he found the door of the Bransome flat open. He went in, noted activity in the studio, and retired to the living-room. Functionaries in conference looked up to stare at him; but he made himself comfortable on the couch, lighted a cigarette, and waited.

Nordhall came in after a while, saw him, and advanced with a torn fragment of tracing paper in his hand. He said, "I guess you had the right idea. We found this at the bottom of the box. She had a try, anyway."

Gamadge wasn't allowed to handle the fragment, but Nordhall held it in front of him to look at. It had a neatly pencilled oblong on it, which was marked off into small squares. There were old English letters in the squares on the left.

Gamadge said: "She was going to trace it over watercolour paper; if she'd managed to finish it. That lettering is tricky, I told you so."

"Do I care? What was tricky was fixing up the valentine. Makes gooseflesh to think of it, don't you say so too?"

Gamadge read:

Behind the
Rainbow
Under the
Cloud
Eternal brightness

He nodded, leaned back wearily against Miss Bransome's cushions, and shut his eyes.

CHAPTER TWENTY

Best Motive of All

"I DON'T KNOW myself, exactly," said Bishop, "but I figured you out as a smart guy, and a kind of a pleasant guy too. And you were on the sidelines, no bets on anything."

He sat on the chesterfield in Gamadge's library, one of Theodore's best juleps in his hand; dressed conservatively enough in dark blue to have satisfied even Bruce Dunbar's taste. He sat straight up in his corner, self-contained and serious of mien as usual, but with amusement in his eyes.

"I'm afraid I didn't do the errand very well," said Gamadge. "I was too tired. But I realized you were on a spot, and as I had already decided, as I explained to you, that you were not Fuller—"

"You did fine," said Bishop, smiling. "All I wanted was to be up on the platform leading the band when the news broke. I thought it would look better. When I heard that somebody had phoned in about finding Osterbridge, I hoped I'd get an opportunity to express my appreciation."

"You expressed it by leaving me out of the picture, and telling Miss Bean to leave me out."

Bishop looked surprised. "You weren't in it. I wouldn't want to make trouble for somebody that had done me a favour."

"I suppose you didn't see the body until you got back from your trip to the bar?"

"Doped that out, did you?"

"I did the stretch from the side door to the gate and back again, yes. On the second trip I acted as I thought you might have done when you came in—I lighted a cigarette, and I just got a glimpse of his white sleeve."

"That's how it happened to me. I went over and looked at him, and I didn't like to leave him there. But this was a frame I didn't understand, and I couldn't afford any part of it. I wonder how Dunbar figured it." He looked at Gamadge over the rim of his frosted silver cup. "Have an idea myself."

"I'd be grateful for it."

Bishop drank, put the cup down, and studied the tip of his cigarette. "I'll tell you if you'll pass it along as yours. It's just a whim of mine, but I never did enjoy the society of those law enforcement boys, and I've had a good deal of it lately."

"Count on me," said Gamadge, laughing.

"I imagined that Dunbar must have been down at the Stanton a good deal, calling on Gail—Mrs. Tanner. He might have been there for lunch; they have it in the garden from June to October, every day that the weather's fine, with the windows into the dance room open so that the customers can hear the band. During the intermissions Osterbridge and I would be very likely to step out of the side door for a gasp of air and a cigarette."

"He certainly may have noticed that."

"So the other night, seeing his way clear past the parking lot feller, he might take a look. If he didn't have any luck, he could go home, come back again later, and follow Osterbridge back to his place. If Osterbridge took a cab, he could even go up and pay him a call; or have another try another night. As I understand it, it wasn't life and death for Dunbar; just setting up somebody to take the rap."

"I suppose Osterbridge would walk down to the gate with him, and off behind that tree if Dunbar wanted a talk about—say, Mrs. Tanner?"

"I guess he would."

Gamadge put his hand in his pocket and brought it out holding the black valentine. "Something of yours; they didn't bother with it after they found the sketch for Dunbar's."

Bishop, looking at him with arched eyebrows, took the card; he glanced at the cover, and then inside.

After a pause he looked up again, a curious expression on his unexpressive face. "I guess this must have been an order."

"It was."

"I heard something about it from—I heard something. Funny kind of thing for me."

"She was civilizing you," said Gamadge.

"Yeah, guess so." Bishop leaned forward to hand it back. "You take charge of it."

"Not interested?"

"Well no; and if you won't be shocked at me, I'll say I never was."

Gamadge took the inside leaf out of the valentine and held his lighter to it. When it was burned, he said: "The other one was from the heart. Two fixed ideas, Bishop; they call that mania."

"His must have been easy money."

"It was. We know what hers was. All he wanted was money and the good life, and he killed to get it. All she wanted was everything she had never had, and without him would never have again. She killed because it was the only way she could keep him." Gamadge looked down into the icy depths of his drink. "I had a talk with Mrs. Tanner after he was dead. She says she thinks her sister got the final push towards murder that day she disappeared—at lunch, you know. Dunbar came in, and Mrs. Tanner says he said something to Alice, she won't tell me what. She thought at the time it must just be a joke, but now it seems to strike her as having been frightful."

"She fixed him up afterwards," said Bishop. "The Dunbar girl did. What could he do? She was out to get him, and she might turn crazy enough not to care what happened to her.

Anybody can kill anybody if they don't care what happens to them later."

"And he couldn't very well appeal to the law or to her family. Which gives him," said Gamadge, "as good a motive for murder as there is."

"They say self-preservation leads the list." Bishop finished his drink and rose. "Have to be getting along... What did he sing out like that for—at the Stanton?"

"That's the way people like Dunbar let off steam. Soothing to the nerves, soothing to the vanity."

"Nice melody."

Outside the library they met Macloud on his way in. Gamadge introduced the two, and went down with his guest to the front door. When he came back Macloud was waiting for him, drily smiling.

"Bishop was kind enough to suggest coming up and talking something over," said Gamadge. "Have one of these."

"They look good," said Macloud, as Gamadge poured from the jug. "Theodore's hands evidently didn't tremble, but he seemed a little perturbed when I came in. Thinks you're collecting exotics. Bishop seemed at home."

"Very sympathetic character. He hasn't had his vacation yet. Needs a rest, and I don't think he'd mind saving money; I wonder if he wouldn't like it up at our cottage."

"Don't push Clara too far."

"Wait till she hears that Jennings now has a means of ingress. She'll leave me."

Want more Henry Gamadge? Read the first chapter of the next book in the series, *Death and Letters*

DEATH AND LETTERS

CHAPTER ONE

Crossword

THERE WAS A row of narrow casement windows across the east end of the bedroom, and a sash window, broad and high, in the north wall. The middle casement window was partly open, the sash window shut tightly and screwed down.

To the north old trees, barely in leaf, screened the view up-river; to the east the grounds were cut sharply off where the cliff ended. A pale, cold April light, subdued by grey skies, came into the room bleakly. It was a comfortable, almost a luxurious room, but it had a clumsy, cluttered look to modern eyes; it was old-fashioned in an unfashionable way. It had an oriental rug on the floor, a gilt-framed oil landscape over the chimney piece, thick silk curtains, pottery lamps with silk shades, ornate wooden furniture, a double bed. Logs burned in the fireplace—it was a cold afternoon.

A nurse in uniform sat beside the north window, doing a jigsaw puzzle. She was a squat, dark woman, and the sharp lights from her cap and dress brought out greenish tints in her sallow skin. She had the bulging forehead of obstinacy, and there was strength in every motion of her short arms. She must have known that she was not much to look at, and perhaps she thought that that was why her patient sat with her back turned;

perhaps that was why she cast a sour look at the patient's back, now and then.

The patient had moved her little bandy-legged desk from under the casement windows to the corner next them on the right; it was now under a looking-glass in a painted velvet frame. The patient had said she got the light better that way, and certainly she must have needed all the light there was for her eternal crossword puzzles. She was doing one now, out of a little paperbound book. There were printed forms and business envelopes on the desk-flap, but she had pushed them and the ink and pen tray aside.

She seemed to be making heavy work of her puzzle just now. She filled in squares, rubbed out letters, consulted other diagrams in the book, sat in thought, looked up often at the mirror, which reflected the top of the nurse's cap.

She was perhaps forty years old, and she might once have been a beautiful woman; now she looked pale and worn. She was very thin. Undoubtedly she had had an illness. But her dark hair was carefully dressed, and she was very neat and smart in plain black, with thin black silk stockings and black suède shoes.

The nurse said: "Don't tire yourself out, now, Mrs. Coldfield."

"No."

Mrs. Coldfield watched the cap in the looking-glass, but it wasn't moving. She filled in the last blanks of her puzzle; with dots substituting for the black squares, it looked like this:

THEMA. PLESCLIFF
S.I.D.E.T.H.I.R
DFLOO. RBACKFROM
W.H.A.TCFENWAYH
ASTOLDMEITHOUGH
T.Y.O.U.M.I...
GHTIMAGI.NESOME
W.A.Y.T.O.G.E.T.
MEOUTO.FTHISPLA
...C.E.Q.U.I.E

TLYIDONOTSEETHE
E.N.D.A.N.D.S.H
ALLNEVERH.AVEAN
Y.O.T.H.E.R.C.H
ANCETOCOM.MUNIC

She turned the thin page, and the nurse spoke again: "You going to do another? How they coming?"

The cap in the looking-glass was rising. Mrs. Coldfield turned another page to a half-finished diagram. She said: "Not very well. They're rather hard—for me."

The nurse had come across the room and was looking over her shoulder. She said: "I'd go crazy."

"They rest me."

"Only trouble, they're not sociable. How'd you like to help me with this jigsaw I'm doing? You can talk and do jigsaws."

"I'd like to go on with this for a while."

The patient spoke politely, but without expression. The nurse, disgusted, went down the long room and through a communicating bath to another bedroom beyond. The patient's eyes followed her. She came back with an open box of candy.

"Have one?"

"Not before tea, thank you."

The nurse went back to her jigsaw. Irritating, she thought, how she never calls a person by name; as if you didn't have a name or wasn't there. But you couldn't irritate *her*...not if you tried.

The patient turned a leaf to an untouched diagram. She worked faster now:

...ATECONSULTDRD
A.L.G.R.E.N.F.O
RCASE.HISTORYON
L.Y.M.R.S.Y.E.A.
BLAGDONFO.RBACK
G...R.O.U...N.D.

ONLYNUR.SEHASSU
P.P.E...R.A.T
EIGHTSY.LVIACOL
D.F...I.E.L..D

She glanced up at the mirror, carefully removed the two pages from the book, folded them once, and slipped a stamped, addressed envelope out from under the business papers on the desk. She put the crossword pages in the envelope, sealed it, folded it into one of the printed forms, and fitted both into a long envelope which was addressed in bold type to an industrial company in New York. Then she looked at her wrist watch. Still looking at it, she said in her quiet, expressionless way, "I had no idea it was so late."

"Late?" The nurse looked at *her* wrist watch. "Late for what?" she asked comically.

"The postman will be coming. I must sign these proxies and get them off. Date them, too; it says so." She picked up a card. "Date them. What's the date, I wonder?"

"It's Easter Monday," said the nurse, "April the eighteenth." She got up and came over. "You shouldn't be bothered with business."

"You heard my brother-in-law ask me to do them." The patient was signing busily.

"Is there any rush?"

"There is, by what they say."

The nurse was not likely to read the fine print on those mysterious cards and letter-sheets, and she accepted the probability that rush was a part of business. She stood while her patient blotted the forms and put them in their envelopes. When they were ready she picked them up and licked the flaps. The patient sat without looking at her, motionless—entirely motionless; she was holding her breath.

When they were all sealed, Mrs. Coldfield suddenly leaned forward with her elbows on the desk-flap and her head in her hands. The nurse stood looking at her sharply.

"You tired yourself out, just like I said. Now don't do another thing before tea."

"I hear him on the gravel."

"Such ears I never—you can't hear him all the way around to the front."

The nurse walked over to the door, was about to push the button of a bell, glanced back at the figure bowed over the desk, and raised and dropped her shoulders in a skeptical kind of shrug. She looked at the casement—a cat could get through that half-opening, nothing much bigger would make it. She went out, locked the bedroom door behind her, and descended two flights of stairs. When she came back the patient was sitting in an armchair, her head back, her eyes closed. She looked quite peaceful.

"Mustn't brood, you know," said the nurse brightly.

The patient opened her eyes slowly and looked at the other woman.

"Have to be cheerful to get well." The nurse switched on two of the lamps. "Tea's coming."

"Doctor Dalgren said I was well."

The nurse frowned heavily. "It's Doctor Smyth's case now."

"Of course. Silly of me."

"How about tea downstairs? Make a change." She added: "They're all out, every last one of 'em."

The patient smiled. "Yes, I know."

"That party at the Watertons', that ought to be something! Too bad you had to miss that."

"In any case I couldn't have gone. I'm in mourning."

The nurse, taken aback a little, said after a pause: "Well, it's only a family party after all. It's all right for them to go to that."

"It's all right to go to anything, if you feel like going."

"That's what I say. Come on now, take an interest; let's go downstairs for tea, and then out for a walk."

Mrs. Coldfield said as if in slight surprise: "But what if callers came?"

This was in bad taste, execrable taste. The nurse said stiffly: "They won't come in the library—Mr. Ira's little library." She added: "You're not well enough to see strangers."

"I can see that it wouldn't do."

"Now don't be naughty. I want to tell the doctor that you're ever so much better."

Mrs. Coldfield turned to look at the nurse steadily. She asked: "Well enough to travel?"

The nurse returned the look. There was a question in her eyes, too. But after a moment she said loudly: "Doctor Smyth is a very experienced man, he has a big reputation in this vicinity. All the big people have him, and he has ten times the medical knowledge of these psychiatrists."

Mrs. Coldfield leaned back again. She said: "I'll have tea upstairs, if you don't mind."

"I won't take hold of your arm."

There was a long silence. Then Mrs. Coldfield turned her head again, met the nurse's eyes, and smiled. She said: "If you did I should understand."

The nurse thought: She's a smart one. It's none of my business, Smyth knows his job. But what did she *do*?

If you're curious about other books
in Felony & Mayhem's
Vintage Category,
take a look at the
first two chapters of

Skeleton Key
by Lenore Glen Offord

SKELETON KEY

CHAPTER ONE

The Mad Professor

THE STREET SIGN appeared first, like a ship's mast coming over the horizon. *Grettry Road*, it read, in black letters on a strip of yellow-painted tin. The larger sign below it came into view next, line by line: NOT A—THROUGH—STREET.

The young woman toiling up the hill took in the whole unencouraging message, paused, looked at the steep slope behind her and spoke aloud, indignantly. "My pals!" she said, presumably referring to the city fathers, who might have let her know earlier.

A few more steps, however, brought her to the crest, and the fathers were exonerated. Avenida Drive continued to the right along the edge of a canyon, and the blind street curved downward to the left. Best of all, beneath the signs at the intersection was a convenient flat rock. The young woman made for it and sat down, panting.

She was footsore and warm and on the verge of discouragement. The miniature briefcase she carried was full of magazine-subscription blanks, and as Georgine Wyeth knew too well, they all remained obstinately true to their name. Again she spoke aloud, bitterly; but this time to herself. "You!" she said. "You couldn't sell water to a desert tank corps."

This was undeserved. There had been other June days as warm and lazy as this one, on which housewives had answered their doorbells and listened to her sales talk, and sometimes even fallen for the Magnificent Combination Offer, or the Three Year Subscription for the Price of Two. Today, a sudden wave of sales resistance had nearly overwhelmed her.

Oh, well, thought Georgine philosophically, *probably like everything else it could be blamed on the war.* In a season when Japanese forces roosted on the Aleutian Islands, and when the ocean outside the Golden Gate was muffled in a fogbank supposed by many Bay residents to be solidly packed with enemy aircraft carriers, a slight sense of impermanence might well be felt. She squinted her blue eyes against the glare, and looked at the western horizon. There was the notorious fogbank. You had a fine view of it from this perch.

The view also comprised the soaring towers of San Francisco, two bridges and a number of islands, and almost all the cities on the east side of the Bay. Across the canyon to Georgine's left squatted the red dome of the Cyclotron building, and far below it lay the campus, blocked out in fawn and green, tile-red and white, like a section of modernistic linoleum. Georgine surveyed the miles that were spread soft-colored and glittering within her vision, and thoughtfully nodded. She had lived in Berkeley long enough to realize the paramount importance of this view in the minds of hill-dwellers. It explained the existence of the isolated group of houses that was called Grettry Road.

A faint wind was stirring, gratefully cool on her face and neck. She took off her old Panama hat and ruffled the short brown curls of a war bob, and sighed in relaxation. Her round curly head looked like a girl's, and so did the slim figure in the blue cotton suit and saddle oxfords, but her face was more mature. It was a bit too thin and anxious-looking for her twenty-seven years.

One glance at Georgine Wyeth left you with no more than a vaguely pleasant impression. A second proved unexpectedly rewarding; those who troubled to take it saw her eyes and thought "lonely"; her mouth, and thought "sweet"; and then this increasingly sentimental gaze, having reached her chin, was brought up with a round turn. The set and tilt of the jaw spoke of stubbornness and humor, and more than hinted at a peppery though short-lived temper.

Little by little, as at the moment she sat resting with her attractive legs stretched out before her, her face lost its anxious determination and took on a look of soulful thought. She was wondering if she'd ever get used to cotton stockings. This important question occupied the forefront of her mind; another part was lazily deliberating whether to go home now or to ring just a few more doorbells. The short blind street to her left seemed a poor prospect for sales. It was too quiet, half asleep under the summer sunlight; more than likely nobody was at home.

From the Campanile, far below, drifted the notes of a chime: three o'clock. By sun time, of course, it was only two; mid-afternoon, that little zero hour when the shadows forget to change, when a woman alone in the house becomes suddenly aware of a dripping tap, the tick of a branch against the window. The air was full of the sleepy shrilling and humming of insects. Somewhere across the canyon eucalyptus leaves were burning, and their aromatic smoke, sweeter than incense to Californian nostrils, came floating across the hill. Georgine sat on, dreamily inert. Gradually all conscious thought left her mind, until it felt clean and empty as a house ready for new tenants.

She heard it then for the first time: that thin little thread of music, lonely as a shepherd's pipe on the quiet air. It wasn't mechanical music, for the reedy notes wavered a little on the run in the fourth bar, and stopped and were repeated. So, there was somebody at home in Grettry Road. She found herself wondering what odd sort of person would play Schubert's *The Trout* on a mouth-organ.

It caught the imagination, somehow; mental adventures

like this were distinctly to her taste, which was lucky, since as a mother and wage-earner she could hardly afford to seek any other kind. Maybe, she thought, it would be worthwhile to try that street after all.

Georgine Wyeth stood up, looked at the sign that said NOT A THROUGH STREET, and shrugged. Then, quite willingly, as if enchanted by the tune of the Pied Piper, she stepped into Grettry Road.

There was no telling how far away the music had been when she heard it. She rang first at the two well-built, unpretentious houses that faced each other across the mouth of the street. The doorbells burred unheeded in their quiet depths. Nobody seemed to be at home.

From her resting-place the larger part of the road had been out of sight, curving away behind a high outcrop of rock that took up most of the eastern side. She left the porch of the first house on the west and went downhill, scuffing through the dry sickle-shaped leaves that carpeted a vacant lot shaded by a fine stand of eucalyptus. At the outer curve of this lot she paused, looking down the steep slope of Grettry Road, which could be seen in its entirety from this point alone. At the far end, where the road flattened and widened, a low white-painted fence kept cars from plunging into the canyon. There was only one house on the east side, three-quarters of the way down; but on the west there were four.

Three of them were small, differing so aggressively in detail and ornament as to make it obvious that the same hand had built them all. Their front walks, on three descending levels, led straight onto the street—there were neither curbs nor sidewalks—and their narrow side yards were separated only by thin straggles of hedge. They had a comic look, like white puppies peering over the edges of adjacent stair-steps. Presumably their lower floors were built down into the first slope of the ravine.

The door of the highest one stood ajar, and Georgine could hear someone moving about inside, just out of sight. She rang the bell; its tubular chime sounded so close to her ear that it made her jump.

Whoever was walking around that inner room completely ignored the sound. The footsteps were quick but sounded heavy enough to be a man's. She found herself peering through the screen in an effort to see him. She rang again, and waited; waited a full two minutes.

She stood frowning at the screen for a moment, and then retreated rather slowly to the street and stood gazing up and down its empty length. The technique of ignoring agents had certainly been brought to a fine point in these hills; the residents might as well come out and kick you downstairs!

She was irritated, and found herself rather fostering her annoyance. For a moment there she'd had a decidedly queer feeling, *As if*, thought Georgine, *I'd died and didn't know it, and everyone looked right through me.*

Well, there were other houses. She walked fifty feet downhill and tried the next one. Surely someone ought to answer here, for as she came up a door closed audibly in the depths of the house; but nobody came, and she could not even hear the doorbell.

How quiet this street was! There was no sound now except that of her rubber-shod feet, and its padded echo from the rock wall. Generally in mid-afternoon you'd expect to hear children playing, but there could scarcely be any living in this remote, steep dead-end. The silence gave it a sleeping-beauty quality, for the breeze had dropped and the striped shadows of eucalyptus lay motionless on the buckling asphalt of the pavement. She still hadn't found a sign of her mouth-organ player. The music had stopped just before she entered the road, and now it seemed as if she'd never heard it.

She turned her head suddenly, catching in the tail of her eye a movement in one of the upper houses, as if a curtain had been twitched aside and as hastily dropped into place. So that was it; she must have *agent* written all over her, somehow, and the people along this street were playing possum. She'd done that herself in the past. The realization gave her an obscure sense of relief.

At the lowest of the triplet-houses the bell gave off that indefinable echo that tells you the place is empty. Georgine's lower lip folded softly over the upper, and she glanced about her once more. If she had any sense, she'd go home now, but honor must be satisfied. She compromised by not crossing the street; there was only one more house on this side, the big one at the end, and she would probably draw a blank there, too. If not—she prepared to hand out a sales talk that would fairly batter the listener into acceptance.

The big house had no doorbell. She grasped the knocker with unnecessary violence, intending to shatter the echoes; and before she could let it fall, felt it twitched from her fingers.

The door swung open. A majestic Negro woman, in a black dress and white apron, stood benignly gazing down at her. "Come right in," said the apparition softly. "We been waitin' fo' you."

The well-known sensation of walking down a step that isn't there was as nothing to the effect of this welcome. For a moment Georgine could do nothing but gasp. A reasonless feeling of terror touched her, and was swiftly gone. Then she opened her mouth to say, "You can't mean me!" and caught herself just in time. *Why not?* she thought; *there were characters who simply yearned to subscribe to magazines, and it would be crazy to give up the chance of meeting some.* In dazed silence she stepped into the dimness of a square entrance hall.

The dark lady retreated before her with a stately tread, reminiscent of the chorus in *Aïda*. "P'fessah! P'fessah!" she boomed in her velvet voice, into the rear of the house. "She got here." A far-away shout answered, unintelligibly, as Georgine followed her guide into a small, hot, drab living-room that looked as if nobody ever lived in it.

The African Queen gestured nobly toward a chair. "There's been so many disappointed him," she remarked, "I was right glad to see you comin' along the street, ringin' do'bells. You lose the address?"

There must be a catch in this, Georgine thought. "I—yes," she said vaguely. "People were at home, I heard them, but no one answered the bell."

"Maybe you tried Frey's." The deep voice was respectfully soothing. "He's stone deef. And the Gillespies, next to him, they unhitched the do'bell because Mr. Gillespie works nights."

So that was it; simple, normal, only Georgine hadn't happened to think of it. Yet she gave a nervous start as another voice spoke from the doorway, "That's all, Mrs. Blake," it said, and the housekeeper strode magnificently out.

The Professor was tall, bald and sixtyish. His sharp black eyes, narrowed in the hot glare from the window, looked Georgine over; once up, once down, He nodded, came briskly into the room and sat down on a straight chair. "Your name?" he snapped out.

Georgine's fingers moved toward the clasp of the little briefcase. She usually began by giving her name, though few forestalled her by asking. "Mrs. James Wyeth," she said. Jim Wyeth had been dead for seven years, but to give her Christian name made her sound like a divorcee.

"Mine is Pah-eff, P-a-e-v," said the Professor, adding angrily, "—the last young woman managed to misspell it in four several ways. Accuracy is my one desire.

"Now; I'll tell you at once that I pay by piecework. There are less than three hundred pages, and I will pay one hundred dollars for the job; one ribbon copy, two carbons. You must work here. Not one page, not one line is to go out of this house. Is that understood?"

Out of this speech, delivered in a furious staccato, Georgine really heard only three words: *one hundred dollars*. Around her floated a vague impression that there had been a mistake after all, that Professor Paev wanted some typing done, that there were certain conditions; but that sum of money loomed in her mind like a glittering promise. She could type; she could earn it.

One hundred dollars. It might be hay to some people, but it wasn't to her. It was more than her entire monthly income from Jim Wyeth's insurance, ten times as much as she earned in her best weeks at the subscription business. It would pay off almost all the debt owed to Barby's doctor since last October, and Barby could have a new winter coat after all, and she, Georgine, could draw a few free breaths. With scarcely a pause, she said, "I understand."

It wouldn't take more than ten days, surely. And she had ahead of her two weeks free of responsibility, for that morning she had seen her little girl start off with the family of a kind neighbor for her first vacation away from home. Georgine firmly believed that no child, however delicate, should become wholly dependent on its mother. It had startled her no little to find that the seven-year-old Barby shared this view, but that was beside the point. Everything was falling into place.

Her shock of disappointment was therefore all the greater when she heard the Professor demanding, "Describe your knowledge of chemistry."

Bang went the doctor's bill. "I had it for a year, in—in high school," Georgine murmured.

"How much of it do you remember?"

She sought wildly for some recollection. "There was an experiment where you put sodium in a tank of water, and it ran around. Mine blew up," said Georgine unhappily. "I'm afraid that's all I—"

"Any physics? Bacteriology?"

Bang went the winter coat. "None," she admitted.

"You're hired," said Professor Paev, briskly rising.

Georgine blinked at him. There was something odd about these requirements; but again, for a moment, the hundred dollars seemed to flutter within her reach.

And then the Professor flung over his shoulder, "I will call the Acme Agency and tell them that if you prove reasonably accurate, I shall be satisfied." He was halfway to the hall before her voice stopped him.

"Professor Paev, I'm not from the Acme Agency."

The man stopped short. Then, with a curious deliberation, he closed the door and came across the room to her chair. "Who sent you here?" he said harshly.

"Nobody. It just happens that I can type. I'm slow, but I'm accurate. And if it isn't taking the bread out of somebody's—"

"Who hired you to spy on me?"

"Nobody, I tell you!"

"It's diabolical," said the Professor, breathing rapidly, "but I might have suspected it. Somehow, they must have figured that my experiments were nearly complete. They'd know how much I needed a typist. They should have prepared you better." The high bald head swooped down at her. "You might as well tell me who it was, I'll pay for the information!"

"I think you're crazy," said Georgine, and thrust herself to her feet. "Do I look like a spy? I came here to sell you some magazines, and before I got the words out of my mouth you offered me a job that it just happens I can do! Who wouldn't take it? I need the money, you need a typist. And what on earth would I be spying *about*?"

"Ah," said Professor Paev with a mirthless smile, "you would like to know, would you?"

They stood glaring at each other. Neither moved, but Georgine had a fantastic mental picture of two cats jockeying for position before a fight. If she held this pose much longer she'd burst into laughter.

"This is absurd," she said crisply. "I didn't intend to cheat you. It's a shame, too, when so many typists have disappointed you—but I see why, now."

The Professor's eyes narrowed. He said nothing.

"Before I go, could I interest you in any subscriptions, renewals, gift offers? I was afraid not. Well, good-by."

She heard an odd rusty sound. It seemed that Professor Paev was chuckling. "Wait," he said. "We might come to an understanding. Perhaps—an exchange of references?"

"Did you say exchange?" Georgine paused on the verge of a step. "That's more like it."

"Ah, yes. Someone whom we can both trust. I live alone

here, you see, though Mrs. Blake is always present during the day. But perhaps I should tell you one thing; the consensus of the neighborhood is that I am perfecting a Death Ray in my laboratory."

Georgine gave him a penetrating look.

"I admit," he said blandly, "that I may have given them that impression myself. Indeed, in one sense it is not far from the truth. But you needn't feel any alarm, Mrs. Wyeth."

Dear me, she thought; *that gasp of mine must have been obvious.*

At five o'clock that afternoon Georgine was still at 82 Grettry Road, the home of Professor Alexis Paev; and she was still slightly dizzy and incredulous.

What an afternoon; up, down, up again in spirits; luck handed her, luck snatched away. The voice on the telephone, that of the President of the Parent-Teachers Association of Emerson School, who had fortunately remembered Mrs. Wyeth; the voice saying, "He's quite mad on the subject of science, but harmless every other way. We've known him for years, long before he resigned from the Faculty." From such a respectable source, this should be completely reassuring; but the words *mad professor* carried inescapable overtones: that laboratory in the basement, walled in glass brick, probably full of evil vapors and steaming flasks, and long tubes glimmering with unearthly lights... A death ray, indeed. The old gentleman's jokes were ponderous, he looked odd when he smiled, as if it didn't suit his face... And he'd wanted someone who knew nothing about science, so she was actually sitting here in a hot little south room on the top floor, with one window that looked off into space across the deep canyon, picking away letter by letter, figure by figure, at a seemingly endless stack of work.

Culture medium Penicillium (spp.), she wrote, *adsorbed by norite. Elute with chloroform, distil, take up in ethyl alcohol and reppt.*

Oh, DEAR, Georgine thought; *I can't do this... Yes, I can. I've got to.*

Ten or twelve days of it...the bill, Barby's coat...something to take up the slack of her loneliness while Barby was away. The stubborn insistence that it still came under the head of mental adventure...and the pay to be counted not in nickels and dimes, but in dollars; a hundred dollars to come... At five minutes after five it came, in a lump. The Professor tapped on the door, whisked in and inspected the three pages she had laboriously finished, nodded and got out a check book.

"Not all at once?" Georgine said, frowning at the check.

"All at once. Postdated, you will observe," said Mr. Paev.

She raised grave blue eyes to his. "You're convinced that I'm honest, or will be three days from now?" The long bald head nodded. "And you want to make sure I'll keep coming back until the job's finished?"

"I believe I've read you correctly, Mrs. Wyeth," said the Professor, his gaze doing its best to penetrate her skull.

"I think it's goofy," said Georgine, reaching for the typewriter cover, "but I'm game." The last words fell on empty air. The Professor was already halfway downstairs.

She had to stop work, but she couldn't go home yet. At four o'clock the African Queen had brought up a message; the block air-raid warden was to hold a meeting for all the residents of Grettry Road, even the temporary ones, at five-fifteen, at his home. Would Mrs. Wyeth be good enough to join them?

Mrs. Wyeth supposed she would. After the illogical sensations and unexpected developments of the last two hours, she felt that she could be neither surprised, irritated nor alarmed.

Having got her hands thoroughly inked in the struggle with an unfamiliar typewriter, she now went in search of a bathroom, without bothering Mrs. Blake for directions. There was one on the southwest corner of the house. It was obviously the Professor's own, but he could scarcely object to her drying her hands on one of his paper towels.

How like a lone man immersed in science to build such a house; all the furniture drab, hideous and far from inexpensive, most of the rooms an inconvenient shape, and the best view in the place from an upstairs bathroom! She raised the window and leaned her arms on the sill. You could see all of Oakland, shimmering under the heat-haze of late afternoon; you could see the lion-colored flanks of the bare hills to the south, and the plantations of trees nearer to Grettry Road, and the canyon that fell sheer from the fence at the end, and grew shallower as it swept around to the north past the back yards of the Road, dark with manzanita bushes, blue-green with bay and young gum trees.

And just below the window, you could see a thicket of flowering shrubs, and a spot right up against the house wall where, it seemed, the Professor had begun a garden.

That was a curious place for a flower-bed, hemmed round with bushes so tall that it could be seen only from this spot directly above. There were no other windows that overlooked it, for the living-room wall below was blank at that spot. There wasn't even a path leading to it.

It was a cleared space of earth, recently cultivated so that no weed marred its slightly mounded surface, and it was about six feet long and three feet wide. There was just one thing it resembled: a freshly made grave. The old man couldn't have *meant* that, about the Death Ray?

He was joking, I know he was! Georgine told herself fiercely, clutching the window-sill, unable to avert her gaze from the spot below. *People simply don't murder other people and bury 'em in the back yard. They don't! Probably if I were down on the level ground, that patch would look quite different. It's just being so far above it that makes the thing look so uncanny. That must be it.*

She withdrew slowly from the window. Her fingertips ached from digging into the sill, and it took an effort to erase the frown that tightened her brows.

CHAPTER TWO

Everyone On Edge

IN THE LATE AFTERNOON, it seemed, Grettry Road came to life, for the living-room of the block warden's home, thirty yards up the street, was respectably full ten minutes before the meeting began. Mrs. Blake, who had walked up with Georgine, withdrew in great dignity to an isolated corner. "Hired help," she explained serenely, "ought to sit by itself."

"Doesn't anyone else have help?"

"They used to," said Mrs. Blake. A look of melancholy pleasure came over her ebon face. "They had Japs."

The warden was not yet on hand. Georgine had gathered that he was a bachelor; the woman with the genuinely golden pompadour, who was arranging blinds and showing people their seats with a proprietary air, was only the next-door neighbor, Mrs. Gillespie; her husband, a large, handsome, sleepy-looking man, was also on hand and rather sulkily assisting her.

The golden lady must have been ravishingly pretty, ten years before. The beauty was still there, but beginning to go soft around the edges like an ice-cream shape left too long on the plate. Georgine thought she looked wistful, as if anxious for people to like her; and this impression was carried out when Mrs. Gillespie, sitting down beside Georgine on a large chesterfield, was distantly greeted by the woman on the other end.

"Couldn't you call me Mimi, Mrs. Devlin?" she asked with rather touching shyness. "I mean, all we neighbors know each other so much better, now there's a war on."

Politely, but with no enthusiasm, Mrs. Devlin repeated "Mimi," and thereafter returned to the formal mode of address. She was a large bony woman with the face of a saintly horse, and for the first few minutes she was surprisingly cordial to Georgine.

"You're the Professor's temporary secretary, Mrs. Wyeth? How very interesting. Rather eccentric, isn't he?"

The check rustled in Georgine's pocket. She felt constrained to say nothing, but to smile vaguely.

"How boring for you," said Mrs. Devlin, "to be dragged to this utterly pointless meeting. We've been perfect martyrs to Mr. Hollister's whims. Don't you think this talk about air-raids is a pack of nonsense?"

"Not quite that," Georgine said. "If there really were an air-raid it'd be a big help if we knew what to do."

Mrs. Devlin lost interest in her at once, and turned aside to get the best light on a large square of needlepoint work. "Mrs. Wyeth, this is my little boy," she murmured.

The little boy, who was about six feet tall and looked at least seventeen, flushed painfully at this title. He hastily told Georgine that his name was Frederic, only everyone called him Ricky. "I'd just as soon get 'em started on Fred, or something like that," he added. "Ricky sounds pretty juvenile."

Georgine smiled up at him. She did like these teenagers, so nice and easy without being fresh; they simply acted their age. And what a handsome young sprig this was; he must resemble his father.

Ricky Devlin, having impressed her with his maturity, now suddenly looked about twelve years old. "Are you typing the Professor's stuff, Mrs. Wyeth?" he demanded, his eyes shining. "Gee, listen, is it really a Death Ray?"

"Ricky," Georgine said, "between us, I don't understand a word of it."

His face fell. Probably he was still secretly devoted to Superman comic books. He was about to say something more when a clear, languid young voice sounded at the door, and his head involuntarily turned. "Hi, Claris," he said, elaborately offhand.

"Hi, Rick," the slim creature answered, lowering extravagant lashes over hazel eyes. She might have been sixteen or twenty-two; there was just one word to describe the red-gold hair in its long bob, the little swing of the skirts, the soft mouth as brilliant with lipstick as an enameled cherry on a hat: *luscious*, Georgine thought. What was her name, Claris Frey? Well, Claris was a dish, and no mistake. Somehow, Georgine's generalities about young people didn't quite fit, here. The child looked as if she were trying to be older than her age, an attitude which Georgine thought had died with the post-war flapper.

Just behind her came a tall, graying man with curiously intent eyes and a gentle, deprecatory smile. He might at one time have resembled the gorgeous infant he had fathered, but something had drawn deep lines of patience in his face, pulling it into a brooding mask.

"Claris," Mrs. Gillespie called, "bring your dad over and introduce him. This is Mrs. Wyeth, who's going to be with us a few weeks."

"Just in the daytime," Georgine explained, as the man crossed the room with a graceful light step, and held out a hand with a smudge of green paint near the wrist. Claris had stood directly in front of him, speaking softly but with great precision, and Georgine realized that this must be the "stone deef" gentleman who had not heard his own doorbell; but it scarcely prepared her for the loud bellow with which he greeted her. "I am glad to welcome a new neighbor," bawled Peter Frey, into a sudden silence.

Georgine was horrified to hear herself shouting in return, though she knew it was useless. She wasn't moving into the

Road, it was only by chance that she—in fact, she'd rung Mr. Frey's bell that very afternoon—

His eyes followed her lips with desperate concentration, and halfway through her stumbling speech he began to shake his head. "I'm sorry," he said, this time almost inaudibly. "I started too late to learn lip-reading. You have to go very slowly for me—or maybe you'd write it?"

He was actually pulling out a pocket pad when Georgine's violent head-shakings stopped him. She was crimson and smiling with embarrassment. Peter Frey also smiled, slowly and painfully. He made an abortive gesture, bowed, and left her, standing with his back to the room and looking out the window.

Mrs. Gillespie at once began to talk airily about something else. "Aren't we a funny lot, up here? I'd always wanted to live in one of these hill houses, with a view, you know, and where there were nice people so we could sort of neighbor back and forth." She cast a dubious glance at Mrs. Devlin, and lowered her voice. "They don't seem to do it as much as I'd thought, though. We've been here for nearly a year and a half, longer than Roy Hollister or the Freys, but I never got to know any of 'em except Roy until these meetings began. My brother Ralph that lives with us, he says they're just a bunch of dopes, but I think," said Mrs. Gillespie courageously, "some of 'em would be real nice if you got to—"

She broke off and sat with parted lips, listening. The buzz of general conversation died; from the open street-door down the hall a man's voice sounded, strident, authoritative: "What in the hell have I got to do with it? I pointed out your position, and that was all."

"That's all?" The answer came in a higher key, unsteadily. "You—you keep me on the rack, you won't lift a finger to—"

Mrs. Gillespie half rose from her seat. "Ralphie!" she breathed, and then caught her husband's eye and sank back reluctantly.

"Shut up," said the first voice, in a lower tone, "and come on in to the meeting. If I think of anything I'll let you know, so you can quit doggin' at my heels."

"Ralphie," Mrs. Gillespie whispered again, her hands twisting nervously. "Oh, why will he—"

Abruptly a man appeared in the living-room door, and stood surveying the company. You knew at once that his was the strident voice; he was a stocky man with a florid, unremarkable face, the felt armband of Civilian Defense prominently displayed on his sleeve. It was a good entrance, effective as the sharp rap of a gavel. The audience froze to attention.

Warden Hollister opened his lips to speak; and, sudden and loud as a gunshot, the front door violently slammed.

Everyone in the room gave a nervous start, and Peter Frey swung round from the window. That shattering noise had had in it all the fury that taut nerves could produce.

Mr. Hollister recovered himself and laughed shortly. "Come in and sit down, Stort," he said over his shoulder. After a moment a lean man, somewhat resembling Mimi Gillespie, passed him with averted, twitching face. He sat down wordlessly in a dim corner, beside a man whom Georgine hadn't yet identified, and remained throughout the meeting in the same position, gazing down at his knees, a lock of blond hair falling over his eyes.

"Now," Hollister said, looking around swiftly, "Are we all here? Where's Devlin?"

"Out of town," said Mrs. Devlin shortly. Her son added, "Sure, didn't you notice the Jeep was off the street? I can't keep her in the garage when Dad's home."

"The Carmichael ladies?"

Several voices told him that the ladies were in Carmel, opening their cottage so they could go down for the weekend of the Fourth.

"When they knew there was to be a meeting?" Hollister scowled. Somebody chuckled softly. "Well, damn it, I don't hold these get-togethers for my health, you know! I've got information to pass on, and you're supposed to come here and listen, all of you."

"Heil Hitler," said Mr. Gillespie, just audibly.

The Warden ignored this with an effort, and glared into a corner. "Is Professor Paev absent, *again?*"

Mrs. Blake's organ tones answered him. She would pass on anything important, having been sent as deputy for an employer who never left home if he could possibly help it. "Anyhow," she added, "come some bombs, it'll be my job to attend to 'em. I guess the P'fessah couldn't be bothered." She retired again into her dignified silence.

"Maybe you're right," said Hollister with a grudging smile. He flipped open a notebook. "Now, will you all attend carefully, please. There's a new method of treating incendiary bombs—"

Mrs. Devlin sighed audibly.

The meeting progressed with remarkable efficiency. Georgine found herself thinking that these hill-dwellers were making very heavy weather of their defense measures. In her section, the householders perfected their preparations and then relaxed; up here, everyone was in a state of tension, as if expecting a bomb to drop.

It was the warden himself who was producing the tension. She became increasingly sure of that as he talked. The man was terribly in earnest, everything he said was quite true, but he was scaring people instead of reassuring them. "I want to speak about carelessness in leaving lights on," he said heavily. "You have all been asked to remove the bulbs from your illuminated street numbers. Don't you know that those can be seen for miles in the air, and that an enemy airman is instructed to bomb any light that's showing? If Grettry Road is blown to bits, it might be the fault of just one of those numbers."

"Well, why tell us about it?" said Harry Gillespie defiantly. "We've all fixed ours. It's the Carmichaels you're talking about, as we—"

"The Carmichaels?" Peter Frey burst in obliviously. His eyes had been going from face to face, desperately trying to catch up with moving lips. "Are you talking about them? They're to be away for a few weeks, and they asked me particularly to see that their flowers were all picked; so please take any you want, everybody."

"Daddy!" Claris shook his arm and he subsided, lowering patient eyelids. "If the Professor doesn't have to come," she added, "I don't see why Dad should."

"I appreciate it," said Hollister sharply. "Anything that's done in the way of coöperation is a little bit of help to me. Lord knows I don't get much. Now I've got to watch for the old ladies to come back, and go speak to them about that light. I'm the fall guy. I'm the only one available up here to do the dirty work, and I'm rushed to death as it is."

"Listen, Mr. Hollister," Ricky Devlin said eagerly, "you could use me any time, you know I told you that."

"Now, son," said Hollister impatiently, "we've been over that before. The grown men would all have to be out of the way before they could use you." He added slyly, "You've got business of your own at night, anyhow." Ricky gave him a swift look.

"Yes, Ricky darling," said Mrs. Devlin fondly, "you're far too young, you're just a baby yet."

An agonized silence followed this remark. Everyone mercifully avoided looking at Ricky, but from the corner of her eye Georgine saw his clasped hands tightening until the knuckles glistened. He caught his breath sharply as if to say something, but Mrs. Devlin, all unaware, went on, "And certainly it won't ever be necessary. We haven't even had a blackout for months, and I do think this hysteria is bound to die down soon. We work ourselves up over something that can't happen at all!"

"But it can, Mrs. Devlin," said Hollister grimly, "That's what I keep tellin' you—any night, any minute. What's more, the next blackout is like as not to be the real thing. And let me tell you, when it comes I want every one of you to get in his refuge room and stay there. None of this hoppin' out into the street to look up at the pretty planes, none of this standin' by uncovered windows where you can get glass splinters through your eye."

Without lifting his head from his chest, Ralph Stort said, "Oh, for Chri'*sake*, Hollister."

Roy Hollister's face grew a shade more florid. "Good God, what you people need is to have a few bombs dropped on you! I hope they do fall. You'd obey orders fast enough then. And we've got to be ready. Lord, we're not half covered, up here. We ought to have a day warden, and there's nobody to serve; Gillespie needs his sleep after he's been at the shipyards all night—"

"Damn' good of you to be so considerate," said Mr. Gillespie, in a tone so nasty that Georgine was startled. She began to ask herself, *What goes on in this place?* Wasn't there something more than war nerves—?

"I could serve temporarily, if you like," said the quiet voice of the man sitting beside Ralph Stort. He bent forward as he spoke, and his face came into the light so that its angles stood out like those of a bold carving: eyes deep-set between sandy brows and high cheekbones, flat planes of cheeks, firm jaw. The face looked as if it would be hard to the touch. During the minutes just past Georgine had been watching him as he looked from one person to another, with such a total lack of expression that she'd thought he must be inwardly amused. At this moment their eyes met briefly, and she was sure of it.

"Well, thanks, McKinnon," Hollister said dubiously. "You're night warden in your own district, aren't you? That might do, for as long as you're up here. When are the Cliftons coming home?"

"I don't quite know," said Mr. McKinnon. "I'm not hurrying them, it's very convenient for me to work there daytimes."

"See me after the meeting, then. I guess that's all, folks. If you'd stay a minute, Mrs.-uh-Wyeth? Like you to fill out one of these slips."

Ricky Devlin lingered beside Georgine; she saw that his color had returned to normal, and was no longer afraid that he might burst into tears of shame if anyone noticed him. "Is it you who plays the mouth-organ, Ricky?" she asked. "I heard someone practicing this afternoon."

"Not me," Ricky said. "It musta been Mr. McKinnon over there. He's the old bearcat on the harmonica."

"The one who was just talking? Not *really*?"

Mrs. Gillespie, preparing to go, bent over her. "He's a little queer, anyhow," she said anxiously. "I don't know if he'd be a very responsible warden. You know what he told somebody? They were talking about draft numbers, and he said he'd never be called, the Army didn't want him because he was a Japanese spy. He said they'd fixed up his face with plastic surgery."

Georgine's lips twitched, and she glanced once more at the transformed face, which would have looked perfectly at home under a Glengarry bonnet. "Of course I knew it was a joke," Mrs. Gillespie added, "but he must have a funny kind of mind to say a thing like that."

The living-room was gradually emptying; Mrs. Devlin folded up the embroidery to which she had given her attention throughout the meeting, and looked for her son. He was speaking to Claris Frey. The sight of the two young things standing in a glow of afternoon sunlight brought a queer pain to the heart, but they behaved like no more than casual acquaintances. "New dress, Clar?" Ricky said politely. "Very solid set of threads."

"Thanks," said Claris languidly, turning away to follow her father. Mrs. Devlin gave a little sigh, in which relief and satisfaction were plain. "Coming home with mother, Ricky dear?" she said triumphantly.

It was at that moment that Georgine conceived a violent partisanship for young Frederic Devlin. Anyone could have forgiven him if he had snarled at his mother; but he did not. With a curiously adult resignation he stood back to let her precede him, and there was nothing in his boy's face but courtesy.

Hollister had gone to the door with some of the party, and Mr. McKinnon came strolling across the room to stand by Georgine. The light struck a spark of copper from his sandy brush of mustache. "As one temporary resident to another, Mrs. Wyeth," he said, "let me tell you that all wardens aren't quite as zealous as this one. He does a conscientious job, but maybe we're not so near to dissolution as he makes out." The casual quiet of his voice made light of everything from the war downward.

"I'd gathered that," said Georgine. "This block seems to be organized within an inch of its life."

This innocent remark caused an explosion that made her drop her pencil. From beside the door Ralph Stort shouted, "God, yes! That's a sample of what the authorities do for you, they're not contented with getting us into this goddamned war, they give someone the power to get us in here once a month and torture us. We might as well all be dead. I wish I *was* dead!"

Mimi Gillespie, who had been waiting for him in the hall, now popped back into the room, "Oh, brother, don't say that," she began ineffectually, laying her hand on Stort's arm. At the same moment Harry Gillespie said harshly, "Skip it, Ralph, and come on home. Can't we get through a day without one of your nerve-storms?"

Stort turned on him furiously. "You great hunk of flesh, you don't know what I go through."

"Well, go through it somewhere else," said Mr. Gillespie, vigorously pushing his brother-in-law into the hall. Mimi trotted after them, hopelessly murmuring, "Harry, don't, please. Now, Ralphie, you just need a drink."

"Impassioned," said Mr. McKinnon mildly.

"Right in tune with the rest of the meeting," said Georgine rather crossly. "I never saw a bunch of people so set on annoying each other, or getting embarrassed. And heaven help me, I did my share. Did you hear me in that yelling contest with Mr. Frey?"

Mr. McKinnon nodded, very gravely, but with the twinkle reappearing far back in his eyes.

"Look here," Georgine murmured, "is he as deaf as all that, or is it just convenient?"

"Why?"

"When the door banged he jumped, just like all the rest of us. Were you here then?"

"Yes, I was here. But I think Frey's affliction is genuine. You ever hear of sound perception? The totally deaf can't distinguish words, but they can feel vibrations."

"Oh," Georgine said. "I'm glad to know that; I was just ready to get mad at him all over again, for ignoring his doorbell this afternoon."

"Was that you, ringing at house doors about three o'clock? H'm. I'm sorry I didn't answer, but I was working." He sat down beside her, his light voice flowing effortlessly along. "The morning was one long list of callers: the Fuller Brush man, the last one in captivity probably; and two ladies trying to find out how many extra beds I had, but not with any ulterior motive I believe, and"—he chuckled suddenly, and Georgine looked up—"a little tike about two feet high asking it I had 'any skwap wubbah.'"

Why, she thought, *he's attractive when he talks about something he likes; that kind of amused tenderness makes his face come alive. Funny how much more affectionate the word "little" sounds in a Scots accent that takes the t's out of it.* "Li'le," Georgine murmured inaudibly.

"And so," McKinnon continued, again looking impassive, "I planned to ignore the doorbell from then on. But if I'd known what I was missing..."

He didn't finish, but it was obvious that he was one of those who took second looks at Georgine.

"Maybe it's as well for you," she said. "The way I felt then, I'd have sold you a Magnificent Combination Offer before you could get your breath."

"Sold him a what?" said Mr. Hollister genially, coming in to receive her completed dossier.

"Magazines," she told him. Mr. McKinnon looked over the warden's shoulder and read her address aloud. "Right down in my home district," he observed pleasantly.

"Magazines?" Hollister said, "You're not a secretary?"

"Only temporarily. Professor Paev happened to be looking for one, and I grabbed at the chance."

"Well, well. That must have been what that mousy little gal was after; the one who went in there last week."

"Didn't see her," Mr. McKinnon said.

Hollister kept his eyes on the printed form he held. "Sure. I guess she found the old Prof was too hard to get on with—or something. I only saw her going in that one time. Come to think of it, I never saw her again."

He looked up suddenly, with a jovial chuckle. "Seemed like she just disappeared."

Georgine had thought of Grettry Road as situated at the other end of nowhere, but after all it didn't take so long for her to get home. She could walk it in half an hour, by using the short cut which dropped through the Gillespies' back yard and through the brush and dry grass of the canyon, ending in a breathless scramble up the far side. From then on the streets were steep, but inhabited.

She was tired; she felt thankful for once at the sight of her landlords' house, a job of remodeling which had changed an honest old dwelling into a pseudo-Spanish monstrosity. It was only a few feet from the sidewalk, and Georgine lived in a yard cottage at the rear of its spacious lot. It was lucky that the landlords were elderly and didn't drive, since her house had once been the garage. The approach to it, though now closed by a stucco wall and a very artistic gate, had been the driveway. She went through the gate, under the overhanging balcony lavishly ornamented with pendent baskets and standing pots of petunias, and cast an unhopeful glance at the mailbox. Too early to expect a letter, of course. Barby had been gone only since this morning.

She looked at her check, frankly gloating. In the face of its written figures, she could forget her absurd fancies, the eerie stillness of Grettry Road in the afternoon, the tensions of the warden's meeting, even the curious gardening habits of her new employer.

A year ago she might have regarded the residents of Grettry Road as a queer crew; now, she was aware that they were no more peculiar than the inhabitants of any block in Berkeley—perhaps than a cross-section of a university town anywhere. The know-your-neighbor campaign must have brought surprises to a lot of people.

Georgine put off until after supper the pleasure of endorsing her check and putting it in the mail, addressed to Barby's doctor. The late sunset had died when she slipped out in the warm June night and posted the letter. "There," she said aloud as the green metal flap of the box clanged.

She should have felt triumphant. Instead, an inexplicable feeling seized her; quite against her will, she found herself remembering a horrible story she'd once read. In it, a man had lost the object which could have saved him from doom, and a voice, audible to him alone, kept repeating in his ear, "You can't give it back now. You can't give it back now."

Well, how foolish! Why should she want to give back the check? What if it had passed out of her keeping, almost irrevocably? *You can't give it back now.*

That odd chilly feeling on her shoulder-blades must be due to the fact that she'd run out without a coat. Nobody was abroad on this quiet, respectable street. There was no reason for her to hurry back to her cottage, and close the door behind her and turn on an extra lamp.

But in spite of forcing herself to a moderate walk, she was breathless when she reached the house. Her living-room waited for her peacefully, the same as always in its shabby, comfortable furniture, its brown and tawny colors, the familiar smells of redwood and starched curtains and whole-wheat toast.

She leaned against the door that shut night out, and felt her world swing back to its normal state. This was home, this was sanctuary.